The storm gathered its forces,

streaking the sky with lightning. Curled in the middle of the four-poster bed, Ariana dreamed of a dark-haired magician who wanted to claim power over her.

And because he was so interwoven in the fabric of her dreams, Ariana knew only a sense of inevitability when her lashes fluttered open two hours later in response to a particularly loud crash of thunder.

There on the balcony, silhouetted by a burst of lightning, stood her magician.

And then he stepped into her bedroom....

STEPHANIE JAMES

is a pseudonym for bestselling, award-winning author **Jayne Ann Krentz.** Under various pseudonyms—including Jayne Castle and Amanda Quick—Ms. Krentz has over twenty-two million copies of her books in print. Her fans admire her versatility as she switches between historical, contemporary and futuristic romances. She attributes a "lifelong addiction to romantic daydreaming" as the chief influence on her writing. With her husband, Frank, she currently resides in the Pacific Northwest.

JAYNE ANN KRENTZ

WRITING AS
STEPHANIE JAMES

NIGHT OF THE MAGICIAN

Silhouette Books

Published by Silhouette Books

America's Publisher of Contemporary Romance

SILHOUETTE BOOKS

ISBN 0-373-80694-9

NIGHT OF THE MAGICIAN

Copyright © 1984 by Jayne Ann Krentz

This edition published by arrangement with Harlequin Books S.A.

Visit Silhouette at www.eHarlequin.com

Printed in U.S.A.

One

"Historically it has not been considered wise to insult a magician," Lucian Hawk warned in a dark velvet drawl.

"Are you threatening to saw me in half?" Ariana Warfield demanded with great interest. "Or make me disappear into thin air?" She smiled up at him, smoky blue eyes wide and guileless behind the lenses of her oversized designer glasses.

It was her brother Drake who rushed to smooth over the incipient hostilities which had flared up a few minutes earlier when he had introduced Ariana to the magician. He did so with his usual forthright acknowledgment of what he considered his sister's failings. "Pay no attention to her, Lucian. She's always like this around men of, er, lower financial status." He grinned cheerfully. "She doesn't generally associate with men who earn less than she does, you see!''

''I see.'' Lucian nodded at the revelation, not appearing to be overly surprised. He studied the woman in front of him with a critical, speculative glance, topaz eyes examining her from behind the lenses of his own glasses. Lucian Hawk's frames were not as aggressively stylish as Ariana's. He hadn't opted for the chic aviator look or even the academic style. His glasses were businesslike and very traditional. Strong black lines framed the strange honey-gold of his eyes and matched in color the intense velvet black of his hair.

Ariana, to her horror, was aware of a rush of embarrassed warmth as she endured the gleaming topaz of his glance. Had she insulted the man? In self-defense she turned on her brother, who was two years younger than her own thirty years of age, and therefore fair game as a scapegoat.

''I was not being insulting, Drake. I merely commented upon the rather hand-to-mouth existence which must be the fate of the usual magician!''

''Asking a man why he doesn't settle down and get a decent, regular job is often considered something of an insult,'' Drake shot back dryly.

''Especially when the man is my age,' Lucian pointed out. ''I'm nearly forty, you know. It should be obvious that I'm probably not going to amount to anything more than I already am.'' There was a taunting challenge in his gaze now, and Ariana was vividly aware of it.

"Be reasonable, Ariana," Drake went on, his Warfield blue eyes laughing at his sister. "You didn't come to my party tonight to meet a prospective husband. You came to hire a magician."

"Voilà!" Lucian murmured, sipping from his glass of whiskey and soda. "You see before you one magician for hire. Maybe."

"Maybe!" Ariana swung her narrowed gaze back to meet his. "What do you mean, 'maybe'? Are you interested in the job or not?"

"I'm interested in talking about it," Lucian temporized. "Why don't we let Drake get back to his other guests while we find a quiet spot and discuss the matter?" He took Ariana's arm and nodded at his host. "It's all right, Drake. I'll send for you if the insults start flying too thick and fast for me to stop them on my own."

"Now just a minute," Ariana began waspishly.

But her good-looking younger brother was already trading an easy man-to-man look with Lucian. "Okay, I'll see you both later. Try the den at the back of the apartment, it should be relatively quiet there. Be nice to him, Ari," he advised his sister. "You need him for what you've got in mind. And he's right, you know. It's not generally considered smart to insult magicians!"

Before Ariana could give her brother her views on the subject, he was making his way back into the throng of colorful people that filled his oversized living room. Drake's parties were always full of odd, eccentric, interesting and occasionally fascinating people. He collected them without regard to social or financial status. The only requirement for being invited to one of Drake Warfield's parties was being interesting. Drake was an inventor, and he claimed that he needed these parties to inspire his thinking processes.

He'd tried telling that to the IRS one year, Ariana recalled as Lucian led her firmly through the crowd. But the IRS hadn't agreed to his proposal for writing off the monthly parties as a business expense. As usual, it was Ariana who had been called upon to straighten out the resulting financial misunderstanding.

The masculine hand on her arm was beginning to become annoying, she decided as Lucian guided her toward the doorway. It was a large hand with a supple strength in the fingers, and her arm felt quite powerless in its grip.

"I think I can manage to make it all the way back to the den on my own,' she said dryly, attempting unsuccessfully to release herself. "Would you mind letting go of my arm? You're leaving imprints in the skin!"

Lucian arched one black brow as he glanced down at his captive. "Sorry. Didn't want to take a chance on losing you in this crowd."

"I'm not likely to disappear in the short distance between the living room and the den!"

"A good magician could make you disappear in about two seconds," he pointed out. "But as long as I've got a grip on you, you're safe."

"Thanks!" she muttered caustically. "Are there any other magicians here tonight of which I must be wary?"

"One never knows," Lucian said smoothly.

He whisked her through the doorway, out of the white-on-white living room which had been decorated for Drake by Aunt Philomena. Aunt Philomena redecorated both Drake's and Ariana's living rooms twice a year; not because they liked having their apartments redecorated so frequently but because Philomena loved to do it and Ariana and Drake loved her. It had been Philomena Warfield who had taken them in upon the death of their parents.

For the past six months Ariana's living room had been done in shades of French vanilla and papaya. One of the first clues to the fact that something unusual and disturbing had occurred in Aunt Philomena's life was Ariana's realization two weeks earlier that there had been no discussion of how to redecorate her apartment for the coming six months. But it was the new rash of checks being written on her aunt's money market account which had really alerted Ariana.

If there was one thing Ariana understood, it was money.

Surreptitiously she studied the man who was leading her down the carpeted hall. A magician. Did she really have to get herself involved with this sort of man in order to carry out her plan?

Lucian Hawk stood an inch or two under six feet, she estimated. And he looked the age he had hinted at a few minutes earlier. He was definitely nearly forty.

But it was a hard, tough, streetwise forty, not the slightly paunchy, fading, comfortable forty that seemed to visit softer men. Ariana had a hunch that there had never been much that was soft about Lucian Hawk or his life.

His midnight dark hair was cut relatively short in a casual, controlled style, and there was a lacing of silver in it. The depths of his topaz eyes held a cool, savvy intelligence. Whatever handsomeness the harshly carved face had once held had been transcended over the years by an almost fierce strength reflected in the aggressive line of nose and jaw.

At least he hadn't dressed with the kind of outlandish showmanship one might expect in a magician, Ariana decided thankfully. So many of Drake's eccentric friends advertised their highly individual lifestyles with their clothes. Lucian was wearing a pair of dark-toned cotton twill trousers that rode low on a lean waist, and a buttery-soft suede pullover shirt with an open collar. There was something very right about the suede on him, Ariana thought absently. It went with the quality of rough, virile aggression that she sensed lay close to the surface of the man. A pair of casual leather handsewns on his feet and a rather worn belt completed his outfit.

"Ah, here we are." Lucian threw open a door at the end of the hall. "It looks like whoever did Drake's living room didn't get her hands on his den!" He glanced appreciatively around at the warm, richly comfortable room with its leather and heavy wood furnishings. Then he shot a speculative glance at Ariana.

"Don't look at me," she told him wryly as he released her arm. "I don't do Drake's decorating. I have no artistic talent. Aunt Philomena's the one with that particular ability." She sank down into one of the oversized leather chairs. "Actually, she did do this room, but she did it to Drake's specifications, and when it was finished he made her promise never to touch it again. This is where he does most of his serious thinking."

"I can see why a professional inventor might need a room for that." Lucian smiled slightly as he took the opposite chair. There was something annoyingly casual about the way he settled so easily into his host's chair, as if it didn't bother him at all to make use of someone else's possessions. He looked quite at home on the expensive leather, his legs stretched out in front of him, his arms resting comfortably along the padded sides. There was a lithe, indolent grace about him that irritated Ariana. Where did Drake find his friends, for heaven's sake?

"My brother works hard, Mr. Hawk, even if his hours are a bit irregular," she told Lucian repressively.

He inclined his dark head with an unexpected, almost courtly gesture. "Implying, of course, that I don't work particularly hard?" The topaz eyes gleamed.

Ariana closed her eyes briefly, striving for patience. "I'm sure a professional magician must do something that resembles work occasionally."

"You mean when I'm not sponging off my more financially successful friends like your brother?"

"I didn't mean to imply that you were sponging off Drake!" she shot back coolly. "I know you aren't, as a matter of fact, at least not in any large way. If you were, believe me, I'd be the first to know about it!"

He watched her speculatively. "You keep close tabs on your brother's finances, Ariana?" he finally inquired very gently.

"It's none of your concern, Mr. Hawk, but yes, I do keep an eye on his financial situation."

"Money, I take it, is a primary interest of yours," he drawled.

She shrugged. It was the truth and she saw no point in denying it. "Perhaps we should get on with our business, Mr. Hawk."

"Call me Lucian."

"Fine. Lucian." Ariana nodded crisply and sat forward a little, her fingers laced together in front of her, elbows resting on the arms of the chair. "Has Drake explained any of this to you?"

"He merely mentioned that you're worried about your aunt. And he told me a bit about you," he added thoughtfully, as if he were trying to recall whatever it was Drake had mentioned about her and how accurate the comments had been.

Ariana didn't waste much time wondering what Lucian Hawk's assessment of her was. She had an honest, straightforward impression of herself and knew how she must appear to the magician. Along with her brother she'd inherited the rich cinnamon brown hair of their mother. She wore it shoulder length in a blunt cut, the sides pulled back behind her ears and held, tonight, with two small clips of gold. The look was controlled and chic, and it served to emphasize the wide, aware, faintly wary expression of her smoky blue eyes. The stylish eyeglasses enhanced those eyes, but they also provided a subtle barrier of defense. From behind the lightly tinted lenses Ariana could view the world from some indefinable point of safety.

Ariana had no illusions about her looks. She knew the slightly upturned nose and the gentle line of her cheekbones and jaw needed a lot more purity of shape to be considered beautiful. And the too-vulnerable mouth was another source of dissatisfaction. Ariana did what she could to hide the hints of softness in her appearance by dressing with a sophisticated polish.

Tonight she was wearing a narrow little black wool dress which held the drama of slashed white satin sleeves and a high-standing white satin collar. Delicate black patent leather pumps and dark stockings added to the cool impact of the dress. The sleek line emphasized the slenderness of her figure.

"To put it bluntly, I believe my aunt has somehow come under the influence of a man who claims to be a psychic," Ariana began, her voice laced with the disgust she felt. "Philomena is not a stupid woman—

far from it—but she does have an exceedingly active imagination and she's fascinated with the notion of flying saucers and alien visitations. This character she's involved with is feeding on her interest in the subject, claiming to have had 'encounters.'"

"It's the modern explanation for psychic phenomena," Lucian observed. "In the old days spiritual mediums claimed to be in touch with the 'other side,' the world of the spirits. Now they often claim to get their powers from alien visitors."

"I do not like fraud or deception of any type," Ariana stated grimly, not caring for Lucian's calm acceptance of the existence of psychics.

"It can be entertaining and there's often some very excellent magic involved. If your aunt is enjoying the experience, why not let her do so? Perhaps she doesn't like to view the world from your more, uh, pragmatic perspective."

"If she wants a magic show, she can buy a ticket and go see one! This isn't the same thing at all. I believe this man is taking advantage of her and I want to put a stop to it. I want you to help me expose him."

"You're working on the principle that it takes one magician to catch another?" Lucian's mouth curved wryly.

"Something like that. Can you do it?"

He considered the question. "Possibly. I know you don't have a high opinion of my humble craft, but I am reasonably good at it. How, exactly, is this man taking advantage of your aunt?"

Ariana frowned intently. "Lately there have been some unusual withdrawals from her money market fund. When I mentioned them to her she avoided the question, claiming they were for some unexpected purchases. She's an artist, you see, and she's always involved with new projects."

Lucian regarded her with a mocking expression of wonder. "You certainly do keep track of your relatives' finances, don't you? I hate to mention the obvious, but doesn't it occur to you that your aunt has a right to spend her money any way she sees fit?"

"You clearly have no conception of the sense of responsibility needed to manage money, Lucian," she retorted quellingly. "And, frankly, I don't have the time or the inclination to try explaining it to you. Right now all I'm concerned with is this charlatan who seems to be fascinating Philomena!"

"Are you sure the money she's withdrawing from her account is going to the psychic?"

"I have a strong feeling that it is, yes."

"But you don't know for certain?" Lucian pressed.

"I haven't wanted to pin Aunt Philomena down," Ariana explained, shifting a little uncomfortably. "I don't want her to suspect I'm on to the situation."

"Why not?"

"Because if she thinks I'm suspicious of her new mentor, she won't let me get anywhere near him. We will have to get near him, won't we? In order to expose him?"

"In order to expose him in a suitably impressive

fashion, yes," Lucian agreed. "I hope you realize, though, that true believers often go on believing in their chosen psychics even after most people have been convinced it's all a case of stage magic. I could bring about an elaborate exposé in the middle of one of this guy's performances and still not manage to convince your aunt that the man's not a psychic who's been endowed with special powers from alien spacemen. If she truly wants to go on believing in him..." He let the sentence end with a shrug.

"I understand, but my aunt is an intelligent woman who, I think, will have the sense to see the man for the fraud he is once he's been exposed. Philomena isn't the only one who's been captivated by him, Lucian. Several of her friends are also making weekend trips to his place in the mountains for his so-called seminars."

"Perhaps they're really enjoying themselves," he suggested wryly. "Do you have a right to interfere? After all, it is your aunt's money and time and you claim she's intelligent. What, exactly, is your interest in getting involved?"

Ariana's eyes narrowed as she sat back in her chair. The toe of her black patent leather pump tapped impatiently on the Oriental carpet. "Are you implying I have ulterior motives? That I'm not simply interested in protecting my aunt?" she challenged softly.

"I think your rather overpowering interest in money may account for some of your concern," Lucian admitted blandly. "Presumably your aunt's money will someday constitute your inheritance?"

Ariana almost went white under the implied accusation. For an instant she sat perfectly still and then she was on her feet with a crisp, furious surge of motion, striding for the door.

He was on her before she could wrench it open, catching hold of her wrist in an unshakable grip. How had he moved so quickly? Ariana didn't pause to consider the question. Instead she let the momentum of his grasp spin her around and as she turned she brought her opposite hand up in a quick, short arc that connected effectively with the side of his face.

"How dare you?" she hissed tightly. "You know nothing about my relationship with my aunt and yet you virtually accuse me of worrying about her solely because I'm trying to protect my inheritance! Let go of my wrist, you bastard!"

He didn't release her, but his other hand lifted to touch the reddening mark she had left on his face. The topaz eyes glittered with an anger he was obviously making an effort to control. "Calm down," he ordered in an icy tone. "Calm down and give me a chance to do the same."

"I don't give a damn if you calm down or not!"

"You should," he growled. "I'm furious. It's unwise to insult magicians, but it's downright reckless to make them lose their tempers! Try to remember that, Ariana."

"I'm not going to worry about remembering it because I don't ever intend to see you again. Let go of me before I scream for Drake!''

"He'd never hear you over the noise of that stereo system he's got going in the living room. Come on back and sit down, Ariana,'' Lucian instructed with a sigh of resignation. "I suggest we start over. I shouldn't have implied that you were only concerned about your aunt because of the money, and you shouldn't have slapped my face. But I'll concede I may have deserved the latter,'' he added as he pushed her almost gently back down into the leather chair.

"You most certainly did! Are you apologizing, by any chance?'' Ariana lifted her chin with royal disdain.

"It was not gentlemanly of me to ask about your motives regarding your aunt,'' Lucian said quietly, taking his own seat once more. Something approaching a sign of wry amusement edged his mouth briefly. "But, then, what can you expect from a lowly magician? A man who makes his living with techniques of illusion and deception can hardly be considered a gentleman, can he?''

Ariana stared at him, a little uncertain about his mood. A few seconds ago he had been furious. She'd seen it in the tight lines around his mouth and in the glittering gold of his eyes. Now that the immediate crisis was over she could even admit to herself that perhaps she ought to have been a little frightened for a moment or two. The only reason she hadn't experienced fear was because she, herself, had been so overwhelmingly angry.

"Are you going to accept my apology?" Lucian asked politely.

Ariana drew a deep breath and told him the truth. "Frankly, I doubt if I have much choice. I don't know where or how I'd find another magician at this late date."

"Don't go overboard with the gracious lady routine," he advised dryly.

"Rest assured I'm not tempted to do so. Not with you."

"Ouch." He winced. "I don't suppose you view yourself as owing me an apology?"

"For slapping you? You said yourself, you deserved it," she reminded him spiritedly.

"Just the same, I suggest you don't make a habit of slapping my face every time you lose your temper with me."

"More warnings about angering magicians?" she murmured with apparent interest. Inwardly she was beginning to ask herself if she had, indeed, gotten off lightly this time. The man, as he admitted, made no claim to being a gentleman and there was an aura of rough, steel-edged temper about him that should have cautioned her.

"I can see you don't take my profession very seriously," he retorted.

"Only when a member of it gets in my way or the way of someone in my family," Ariana said pointedly. "Believe me, I take my aunt's new acquaintance very seriously!"

"Don't classify me with that psychic your aunt's involved with!"

Ariana bit back a comment to the effect that all magicians, illusionists and deceivers were pretty much the same to her. But nothing would be served by further insulting the man, and right now, like it or not, she needed his cooperation. He must have seen the flicker of thought in her eyes, because Lucian smiled with a certain grimness.

"Very wise," he applauded in a low, velvety growl.

"Are you going to claim you can read my mind?" she scoffed irritably. "That you knew what I was thinking just then?"

"Any man sitting where I am right now would have known exactly what you were thinking about him. But, then, you're really not making much of an effort to conceal your opinion of me, are you?"

This was getting them nowhere. "Lucian," Ariana began in a determined, steady voice, "I think you were right a few minutes ago. We'd better start over. Let's accept the basic fact that you think I'm mercenary and that I have a few reservations about your chosen profession. All I want with you is a business relationship and I'm willing to pay well for your particular expertise. Will you help me expose the psychic with whom my aunt is involved?"

Lucian propped one elbow on the arm of his chair

and rested his chin on his palm, his pose pensive. "Strangely enough, I'm tempted."

Ariana arched one cinnamon red brow behind the frames of her glasses. "I can't tell you how grateful I am," she said with exaggerated politeness.

"Don't get me wrong, what's tempting me isn't your kind offer of honest employment."

"No?"

"No. It's just that I'm intrigued by the thought of watching another magician in action and seeing if I can figure out how he's operating. I suppose you could call my interest in your offer a form of professional curiosity. I can make no guarantees, however, you do understand that? There is always the possibility that the man's so much better at his craft than I am that I won't be able to expose him. There is also the possibility that when I actually see him in action I'll decide that he's not really doing anything wrong, in which case I will *choose* not to expose him. A matter of professional ethics."

"You don't think it's wrong for a magician to use his skills to fleece my aunt and several of her friends?" Ariana demanded.

"If that is, indeed, what's happening, I'll do my best to put a halt to it."

For a moment Ariana regarded the man she was coming to think of as an adversary. "And how much do you consider fair payment for a job of this nature?" she finally asked coolly.

"You're in luck. The food stamps came in yesterday and I'm feeling generous. I won't charge you a cent," he drawled.

"That's quite unnecessary," she snapped. "I'm prepared to pay for your services."

"I, however, am not prepared to receive money from you," he snapped back, getting to his feet with a sudden lithe movement. She watched as he paced across to the bay window and stood staring out at the San Francisco skyline. What was he thinking now?

"Lucian, I see no reason for this particular argument. It was understood from the first that I wanted to hire a magician."

"Think of the bargain you're getting," he said a little too pleasantly.

"I'm not interested in a bargain magician," she responded behind him, and for the first time her sense of humor rose to the occasion. "They say you get what you pay for and I want the best."

He swung around and was in time to catch the trace of genuine amusement that touched her soft mouth. For an instant he seemed fascinated by the sight. "I guarantee I'll give you my best work. You don't have to worry about that. But I have this strange feeling that any man who gets involved with you had better make it clear from the start that he is putting the relationship on an equal footing. I think, Ariana Warfield, that if I actually accepted your money and went to work for you, you'd make my life hell. Therefore, our arrangement will be a partnership or you can forget the whole idea."

Ariana caught her breath at the absolute finality of his tone. He meant it, she realized. He had no intention of taking money from her and thereby putting himself at her command. Magicians, it seemed, had their share of pride. "All right," she agreed hesitantly, "if you're sure that's the way you want it."

"It is."

She got to her feet. "Very well, then, it's a deal." She glanced at the thin gold watch on her wrist. "We'll have to discuss the details later this week. Right now I'm late for an engagement and I had better be on my way. When would you like to get together to go over what information I have?"

Lucian flicked a hand uncaringly. "Tomorrow evening, perhaps? I'm afraid I'm going to be busy during the day," he said carefully, watching her intently.

"Tomorrow evening will be fine." Ariana nodded once in relief and satisfaction that at last matters were beginning to progress more smoothly. "Why don't you come by my apartment around seven o'clock?"

"Before or after dinner?" he inquired blandly.

"During," she told him crisply, moving toward the door. "And you can leave the food stamps at home. I'll feed you for free. It's the least I can do if you're going to donate your services to the cause!"

"Thank you," he said, moving silently behind her so that it was his hand which went to the doorknob first, not hers. "Where are you headed this evening?"

"I'm going to catch a cab to Chinatown. I'm meeting someone there for a late dinner," Ariana explained as he opened the door for her. She thought of Richard waiting for her and stepped briskly out into the hallway. It was getting late.

"Have you called the cab?" Lucian paced beside her down the hall toward the noisy living room.

"Yes, I phoned earlier and arranged for it to meet me out in front in a few minutes. I'll get my coat and be on my way."

"I'll come with you," Lucian said flatly, drawing to a halt at the closet in the tiled foyer. "Which coat is yours?" He was already reaching for a rugged-looking black jacket with a corduroy collar and metal clasps.

"The white cashmere," she told him, nodding at the elegantly simple coat hanging to one side. "Listen, there's absolutely no need to escort me to Chinatown," she went on quickly as he helped her into the coat. "I'll be perfectly all right. Richard will be waiting for me at the restaurant."

"I know you don't think much of magicians' manners, but we do lay claim to a few," Lucian informed her as she finished tying the sash of the coat. "Besides, I was about ready to leave, anyway. I'll simply go on home after letting you off in Chinatown. Convenient."

"Oh," she paused, seeing the logic of the situation. It would be easier for him if he didn't have to call a second cab. "Very well, if you're sure you're ready to leave."

Lucian looked up as a particularly raucous laugh

filtered into the foyer. His mouth crooked wryly. "Believe me, I'm ready. In a few more minutes someone is sure to start yelling for me to perform a little magic, and since my powers don't extend to making the whole crowd disappear, I think I'll take the easy way out and just make myself disappear."

"Hey, you two, going somewhere?" Drake materialized in the doorway, a glass of champagne in one hand, his other arm around an interesting woman with blue and green hair.

"I'm going to escort your sister to her next appointment and then go on home myself. I'll see you soon, Drake."

"Did you and Ariana come to some arrangement?"

"Oh, yes. We traded a few insults, she slapped my face, I apologized and we agreed we have the perfect basis for a working partnership," Lucian said smoothly as he finished fastening the clasps of his jacket and reached for Ariana's arm.

Drake nodded happily as he watched the other two move out into the chill, foggy night. "Sounds like a solid beginning. Good night, Ari. I'll give you a call tomorrow, okay?"

"Fine. Good night, Drake." Ariana eyed the blue-and-green-haired woman, who smiled back cheerfully. Then the door closed as Lucian firmly pulled it shut behind him. The cab was already waiting at the curb.

"Does this Richard person who's supposedly waiting for you so patiently know about your plans to expose the psychic?'' Lucian asked as he bundled Ariana into the back of the cab and shut the door.

''No, I haven't told anyone except you and Drake about the situation.'' Ariana wondered why she found herself so aware of the way Lucian seemed to dominate the close confines of the cab. With the dark, masculine jacket, that silvered black hair and those topaz eyes, Lucian Hawk definitely constituted a somewhat overpowering presence in the small space. She moved a little uneasily, seeking her own corner of the seat. When she realized what she was doing, Ariana scolded herself silently. She certainly wasn't going to let this man intimidate her!

''Is Drake as worried as you are about your aunt?''

''No, but he agrees it would probably be wise to check out this psychic,'' she told him vaguely, turning to gaze out the window at the city streets. The fog was close tonight, wreathing the street lamps in an eerie golden glow. In the distance a foghorn sounded, and all at once Ariana shivered for no apparent reason. She turned back abruptly and found Lucian's cat eyes studying her intently. A perfect night for a magician to be abroad, she thought fleetingly and then firmly dismissed the fanciful image.

Nevertheless, it was something of a relief to see Richard Dearborn waiting patiently outside the expensive Chinese restaurant he had chosen for the evening. His pale blond hair glistened in the garish lighting of the busy Chinatown streets, and his stylish trenchcoat was belted with a rakish air. A handsome, well-mannered man, Ariana told herself. Not a rough, potentially dangerous magician. The cab drew to a halt and Ariana put her hand on the door handle.

"Goodnight, Lucian, I'll see you tomorrow evening."

"I don't have your address," he noted calmly, his gaze on the man approaching from the sidewalk to meet Ariana.

"Oh, yes, of course." Quickly Ariana dug a business card out of her small black handbag. On the front in engraved lettering it read Warfield & Co., Financial Planners. Hastily she used a delicate gold pen to jot down her address. "There you go." She handed it to him.

"Thank you," Lucian said gently, taking the card. He was still watching the blond-haired man who was leaning down to open the cab door. The driver was getting mildly impatient. "It's nice of you to invite me to dinner, Ariana. I mean, considering your opinion of me and all," he murmured.

She bit down on her lower lip and said quickly, "Yes, well, I'm afraid we're going to have to get accustomed to the idea of getting along with each other. You see, there are a couple of details about this situation I haven't had a chance to explain yet."

"Such as?"

She sucked in her breath and said very hurriedly as she opened the door, "Such as the fact that the only way I'm going to be able to convince Aunt Philomena to let us attend one of her psychic's sessions is to make her think you're a new, uh, close friend of mine."

That caught his full attention. At once the topaz eyes went from the waiting man on the sidewalk to her suddenly tense features. "I'm going to pose as your lover?" Lucian asked harshly.

"I'll explain everything tomorrow night!" Hastily Ariana extricated herself from the cab and almost stumbled with relief into Richard's arms.

The cab door slammed shut, and the driver shot away from the curb without a second's pause.

Lucian found himself staring out the back window, one arm along the seat, watching as Ariana disappeared into the restaurant on the arm of her escort.

Was that man with the pale hair and the three-hundred-dollar trenchcoat her real lover? More to the point, why the hell was the notion so strangely disturbing? Face it, the real reason he'd insisted on sharing her cab this evening was because he had been very curious to see the man she was rushing off to meet. Ariana was both an infuriating and an intriguing woman.

Lucian settled back against the seat as the cab left Chinatown behind and headed for the next address the driver had been given. His passenger glanced down at the engraved business card in his hand and thought about what it would be like to be Ariana Warfield's lover.

Two

Richard Dearborn was not Ariana's lover. He'd made it clear that he would have liked the role, but Ariana wasn't particularly interested in casting him in it. After the "disaster" of her twenty-sixth year she never again intended to be swept off her feet by something as dangerous and unreliable as a man's passion.

The price was far too high, and if there was one thing that Ariana had a talent for, it was analyzing costs.

On the other hand, she was more than prepared to consider marriage—much to the chagrin of her small family. Philomena and Drake made no secret of the fact that they thought her overly cautious and far too practical where men were concerned. What she needed, they insisted, was a wild, blazing affair to wipe out the memory of what had happened when she was twenty-six. They very much feared that life was passing her by.

A wild, blazing affair, however, was definitely not in the picture as far as Ariana was concerned. A stable, comfortable marriage was what she needed now.

Ariana reflected on the situation the following evening as she went about the task of preparing dinner for her newly acquired magician. Richard Dearborn had everything she needed and wanted in a man. He not only made as much money as she did, he made considerably more. He had a sterling reputation as a gentleman and a businessman. He came from a family that had been quietly successful for three generations in San Francisco, and he had proven his own native ability when he had assumed the reins of the family banking business three years earlier. At thirty-four he had shown himself a worthy successor to his father.

And being a solid businessman as well as a logical person in every respect, Richard would understand Ariana's unshakable insistence on a prenuptial agreement if she were to marry him. After all, given their respective financial situations and the practicality of planning for the uncertainties of a modern marriage, a contract made perfect sense. It would protect him as well as her.

Ariana's expressive mouth curved wryly as she popped the walnut torte she had just finished making into the oven. Yes, if and when the time came, she would present the idea of such an agreement to Richard in the context of how it would protect *him*. That approach should work well on a banker.

Heaven knew she didn't want to have to explain that she was the one who needed to have the psychological security of a marriage contract. With a small sigh of self-disgust she slipped off her apron and headed for the bedroom in order to dress for dinner. Explaining her own deep-seated need for an iron-clad agreement would only resurrect the humiliation and financial disaster which she had gone through at the age of twenty-six. That had been the year when she'd thought she had it all: Success and the man of her dreams.

The man of her dreams, however, had turned out to be a fraud, a charlatan who had destroyed her love and her fledgling financial empire in one fell swoop.

Never again.

It was ironic, she thought as she stood in front of the closet, that tonight she would be entertaining a professional deceiver, a man who had made deception and illusion into a fine art.

Ah, well, she needed such skills if she was to deal with the dangerous situation in which she suspected her aunt had become involved. What were the old sayings on the subject? One fought fire with fire. And there was something to the effect that it took a thief to catch a thief. She needed a magician to expose another magician.

At least Lucian Hawk was honest about his chosen vocation, she acknowledged as she selected a pair of narrow black velvet trousers. She didn't particularly admire his choice, but she was in no jeopardy from his magic. Almost absently she pulled out a full-sleeved silk blouse done in a rich amalgam of jewel tones. The ruby, sapphire and gold colors were vibrant against the dark velvet. A pair of black ballet-style slippers finished the outfit.

She brushed her cinnamon-colored hair back behind one ear, catching it with a clip, and allowed the opposite side to swing free. The chic frames of her glasses were a strongly accented accessory in and of themselves, and she decided not to wear anything else in the way of jewelry.

How, exactly, should she handle Lucian Hawk tonight? Ariana frowned consideringly in the mirror as she checked her appearance one last time. She'd startled him last night with that parting comment about having him pose as her "close friend." He'd understood the euphemism at once. Of course, magicians were reputed to be clever people, she reminded herself with an amused smile.

The flicker of humor faded, however, as she walked back into the kitchen to finish dinner preparations. Just how clever was Lucian Hawk? Smart enough, apparently, to refuse to take money from her. She reluctantly gave him credit for that piece of insight.

He was quite right. It would have been easier to control him if he were directly in her employ. Something about the exchange of money for services rendered gave the employer a strong element of advantage over the employee. There was a subtle form of power involved in that sort of relationship, and Ariana would have felt more comfortable and in control if she had been allowed to exercise it.

As matters now stood between herself and Lucian she would be dependent on persuasion and cooperation.

The first thing she had to persuade him to do was act out the role of a man with whom she was having a "meaningful relationship." Philomena was bound to be suspicious of almost any other explanation for a man accompanying her niece to the psychic's next session. For that matter, the so-called psychic was probably going to be damn suspicious, also.

A magician. She'd have to think of some other profession for Lucian when she introduced him to Philomena. Something respectable.

Her doorbell chimed right on time half an hour later. Ariana walked through the warmly decorated living room to answer it. It was a charming room. There was no doubt about Philomena Warfield's being an extremely talented woman. When it came to mixing colors and textures, few could match her. The papaya-shaded carpet made a dramatic backdrop for the vanilla-colored furniture. Each item in the room had been selected for both comfort and style, and there was an overall sophistication about the blend of Queen Anne and French designs. The resulting atmosphere perfectly suited Ariana's lifestlye just as the sleek, ultramodern look of Drake's apartment suited his rather unusual way of living.

"Good evening, Lucian," Ariana began with cool

formality as she opened the door. "You're very prompt."

"I generally am for a home-cooked meal," he said as he stepped inside. Dressed in dark slacks and a deep green pullover sweater, Lucian looked casual and at ease. He slipped off the metal-clasped jacket, the same one he had worn the night before, and handed it to her to hang in the hall closet.

Ariana took advantage of the small distraction to adjust to his dark presence in her warm pastel living room. The fog had left a trace of dampness on his black hair, and he seemed as large and faintly intimidating as he had seemed the night before in the cab. It wasn't that he was an unusually big man, but there was definitely something about him that made her uneasily aware of his presence. By the time she had completed the job of hanging up his heavy coat, however, Ariana had herself firmly under control.

"Thank you for coming, Lucian. Please have a seat. What would you like to drink?"

Instead of obeying her casual wave toward the Queen Anne sofa, Lucian fell into step behind her as Ariana walked into the open kitchen. He slid onto a stool on the opposite side of the breakfast counter as she opened a cupboard full of glasses.

"Whatever you're having will be fine."

"A glass of Johannesburg Riesling?" she inquired, opening the refrigerator to remove the Napa Valley white wine she had been chilling.

"Fine." He watched her.

"I don't suppose you'd like to help me economize

by doing some nifty trick like turning my tap water into good Riesling instead of making me use up this expensive stuff?'' Ariana asked pleasantly as she set the bottle on the counter and searched for a corkscrew.

"You don't look as if you have to worry about economizing to that extent," Lucian remarked with a significant glance at the expensively furnished apartment. "But I will offer to get that cork out of the bottle for you."

She handed him the wine bottle. "With magic, or do you need the corkscrew?" she inquired interestedly.

"I thought I'd just use my teeth," he growled. Then he held out his hand demandingly. "Of course I need a corkscrew. What is this? A test?"

Ariana smiled very brilliantly, handing him the implement. "It's just that I haven't met many magicians and I wasn't sure what to expect."

"We're even then. I'm not quite sure what to expect from you, either." Expertly he began uncorking the bottle. "So suppose we start satisfying each other's curiosity. Why will I be posing as your lover?"

Ariana winced at the blunt question. "Not my lover, Lucian," she qualified. "Just a man I'm currently dating. Someone with whom I have a relationship. Enough of a relationship that my aunt will accept you without suspicion when I ask to bring you along to the séance or whatever her psychic calls his little get-togethers."

Lucian made a noncommittal sound as he removed the cork from the bottle.

"I can't very well tell her who you really are or expect her to welcome you with open arms, now can I?" Ariana went on determinedly. "Furthermore, that damn psychic will undoubtedly forbid you to attend the session if he knows who or what you are. He's not likely to want another conjuror watching him at work, is he?"

Lucian poured the wine, a thoughtful expression on his hard face. "Okay, so you need a reasonable excuse for bringing me along. Who else besides us knows what you're planning?"

"Just Drake."

"How about the man you met outside the restaurant last night?" Lucian asked quietly, handing her a glass and sipping at his own.

"Richard?" Ariana frowned. "No, I don't think I'll tell him what's going on. It would be a little embarrassing to explain."

"You mean about having me as a lover?" he drawled, topaz eyes narrowing assessingly.

"About Philomena having fallen for a psychic," she corrected smoothly. "I'd rather keep this within the family as far as possible."

"I gather from something Drake said last night that he and Philomena and you comprise the total Warfield family, right?"

"That's right," Ariana agreed evenly, leading the way back to the living room. Enroute she scooped up a silver dish laden with eggs which had been stuffed and decorated with caviar. "Our parents were killed when Drake and I were small. They were botanists. Very brilliant botanists, as a matter of fact. They died on a field trip up the Amazon." Her tone made it clear that she did not want to discuss the matter further.

Lucian ignored the tone. "Scientists, hmmm?" He helped himself to several of the stuffed eggs as he sprawled casually on the sofa. "Let's see. Drake is a highly ingenious and successful inventor, your parents were scientists and Philomena is an interior designer and artist of some renown. Your family seems to have more than the normal share of talent."

Ariana shrugged and munched a canapé. She had taken a seat across from him with the wide coffee table between them.

"What talent were you blessed with, Ariana?" Lucian asked almost silkily.

"Nothing very exciting or interesting like Drake and Philomena, I'm afraid," she tossed back coldly. "The only thing I do with any competence is make and manage money."

"Which explains your rather extensive interest in the subject." He held up a hand as a spark flashed in her smoky blue eyes. "Relax. I'm not going to start another insult-slinging match. I learned my lesson last night," he added with a wry smile. "Warfield & Company, Financial Planners, I take it, is just what it sounds like? A comprehensive money management and counseling firm?"

"That's correct," she replied stiffly, sensing the

underlying disapproval in his voice. "We sell a variety of financial services to individuals and businesses. The services are designed to help them make money and control what they do make so that it doesn't all wind up going to the IRS. What about you, Lucian?" she demanded firmly, seeking to change the direction of the conversation. "Has magic always been your chief interest?"

"I've loved magic since I was ten years old," he said simply.

Ariana couldn't help the question which immediately came to her lips. "For heaven's sake, *why?*" Her perplexed expression was totally honest. How could anyone truly love deliberate deception?

Lucian stared at her for a moment as if trying to ascertain her reasons for asking. "There's a real beauty in it, Ariana," he finally said quietly. "People respond to it in such a unique fashion. They're charmed by it. It creates a sense of wonder that's unlike anything else. I enjoy mastering the art that is capable of creating that wonder."

Ariana thought about that and then smiled reluctantly. "You sound like Philomena when she discusses a perfect room or Drake when he's working on something especially clever."

"But I don't sound like you when you're making money in an especially clever fashion?" he concluded perceptively.

She shook her head. "No. I've never thought of managing money as an art form. It's just an ability I have. I don't go around instilling wonder and appreciation in people, although I do instill a little gratitude when things go right or someone gets his financial world straightened out.''

"Perhaps you manage to dazzle people in other areas of your life,'' Lucian pursued softly. "In your relationship with the man who was waiting for you at the restaurant last night, for instance?''

Ariana lifted her chin and gave her guest a quelling glance. "You seem rather fascinated with Richard.''

"I'll admit I'm a little curious about him,'' Lucian said honestly.

"Why? He has nothing to do with this.''

"That's one of the reasons I'm curious. What would he say if he knew you were feeding me dinner tonight and that you're planning to have me pose as your lover?''

"Not my lover,'' she repeated automatically. "And you don't have to worry about Richard. Please forget about him!''

"Does that mean you're not going to worry about him?''

"Of course I'm not going to worry about him. Why on earth should I?'' she snapped. Somehow she had to get control of this ridiculous conversation.

"Then he's not your real lover?''

"Lucian, I don't know what makes you think you have the right to pry into my personal life like this, but...''

"I just want to be aware of all the potential risks,'' he told her flatly.

"Risks!" She stared at him, dumbfounded. "You're worried about the risk of Richard finding out you're pretending to be my—my *friend,* and taking offense?" She refused to use the word lover.

"There might not be time to explain that I'm only pretending. A man in his position could be forgiven for losing his temper rather quickly if he were to discover that you're entertaining strange males in the evenings. All I'm asking is whether or not he has the right to lose his temper over such an event. Is he your real lover? Because if so, I think you'd better tell him exactly what's going on." There was a steel-edged note in his words that enraged Ariana.

She set her glass down on the table with a crystal clatter and glared furiously across the short expanse of space separating her from the magician. "Let me try and make a few things very clear, Lucian Hawk. First, you have no need to concern yourself with any aspect of my private life. You may rest assured that Richard Dearborn will not descend on you and beat you to a pulp, even if he were to misunderstand the situation. He's a gentleman. Second, I do not need or want your advice on what I should or should not tell him. I'll handle my relationship with him as I see fit!"

"Are you sleeping with him? That's all I'm asking," Lucian growled.

"That's none of your damn business!"

"It is my business! My God, woman, if you're having an affair with him and he finds out about me, you're asking for all kinds of trouble. What's the matter with you? Are you so naive that you think he won't care? A man who feels he has a claim on a woman isn't going to take kindly to the notion of said female pretending to be in love with another man, regardless of the situation or reason. And he's going to be even angrier about it if he finds out in a less than straightforward fashion!''

"You speak knowledgeably on the subject!" she flung back.

"I speak from a man's point of view. I know damn well how I'd react if I found out my woman was involving herself in a situation like this without consulting me first!''

For an instant Ariana could hardly speak, she was so enraged. It took the sum total of her willpower to ask far too sweetly, "And what, exactly, would you do, Mr. Hawk? Use your magic to turn the other man into a frog?''

He looked at her with a disconcerting directness that made her catch her breath. She had the impression that he was actually trying to put himself in Richard's place. "I would," he ground out at last, "be furious that you hadn't taken me into your confidence. To put it bluntly, there would be hell to pay.''

Ariana took a savage grip on her temper. "Then it's fortunate you're not in Richard's position, isn't it? For the record, Lucian, Richard Dearborn is the man I may marry. That decision, however, lies in the future. He has no 'claim' on me, as you so chauvinistically phrase it. I assure you, you are perfectly safe.''

Lucian looked down into his wine as if he'd discovered something fascinating floating on the surface of the Riesling. ''If you're thinking of marrying him, you must be sleeping with him. If you're sleeping with him, you're asking for trouble by pulling off this little stunt behind his back. I, as the person most likely to be clobbered in the process, am afraid I must object.''

''I am not sleeping with him!'' Ariana yelped, losing the tenuous grip on her temper. ''There! Are you satisfied? I'm not having an affair with anyone. You're safe, magician. Do you hear me? *Safe!''*

Lucian raised his head once more, and for the life of her Ariana couldn't read the expression in those topaz eyes, but that didn't lessen the impact of his glittering glance. Behind the lenses of his glasses, the honeyed depths of his eyes seemed to burn for a moment and then the fire was gone to be replaced by something much cooler and more controlled.

''I apologize for pushing you so hard about it,'' he said quietly. ''I had to know exactly what I was getting into.'' His voice sounded strained.

Ariana shifted restlessly as she got her emotions back under control. ''Forget it. I just didn't realize how upset a man in your position would be about the prospect of Richard misunderstanding the situation.''

''No,'' he agreed. ''You didn't.''

"Believe me, Richard would not be a threat, even if things between him and me were as you thought."

"I see," Lucian said very neutrally.

Ariana sighed in exasperation. "I don't think you do see but it really doesn't matter as long as you'll still agree to help me in this project."

"Oh, yes. I'll help you. I made up my mind about that last night."

Her eyes widened. "Then why the hell did you just put me through that inquisition?" She got to her feet abruptly. "Oh, never mind. I don't think I want to hear any more of your convoluted masculine reasoning. I'll serve dinner." With a regal, impatient stride she headed for the kitchen and once more he followed. This time he leaned in the kitchen doorway, watching as she prepared to serve.

"I take it that if and when you do decide to marry Richard, you envision a very modern sort of arrangement?" he finally queried in a very conversational tone. He sniffed appreciatively as she withdrew the baked salmon from the oven.

"If you're talking about a so-called open marriage when you say 'modern,' most definitely not. I am a firm believer in fidelity. But if, on the other hand, you're talking about a financially and legally modern marriage, then, yes, I do want a modern relationship," she agreed almost absently, concentrating on arranging the fish on a warmed platter. She could feel his eyes on her as she worked, and wondered at the intensity of his gaze.

"What's that mean?" he asked.

"It means that I would never enter into marriage without such things as a clear and binding prenuptial agreement, for example," she told him, swinging around to thrust the platter into his hands. "Here, make yourself useful and take this over to the table."

"A marriage contract?" He accepted the platter, but his attention was on her as she turned back to the oven for the tray of Duchesse Potatoes. She heard the startled tone in his voice.

"Exactly. A contract protects both parties. It's the only sensible way to go about something as uncertain as marriage."

There was a silence behind her, and when she moved to carry the potatoes to the table she found that Lucian had already placed his platter on the round dining room table. "I take it you don't agree, Lucian?" she smiled, faintly amused. She put down the potatoes and went back to the kitchen for the spinach salad.

"My feelings on the subject are immaterial," he said slowly, holding her chair for her. There was a curious remoteness in his words. "I was married once and I plan never again to repeat the error. Therefore, such modern issues as prenuptial contracts don't arise for me."

He sat down across from her and met her steady gaze. For an instant a strange tension hovered in the air between them and then Ariana broke it with a supremely condescending smile. "So, magician, it would appear we are fated to be on opposite sides of yet another fence. You and I have, apparently, drawn different lessons from our past mistakes.''

He poured out more of the wine and then lifted his glass. "To the lesson I learned,'' he murmured sardonically. "Never trust a woman who says she's in love and wants to marry. She can damn well prove her love by taking the risk of having an affair with me.''

Ariana's chin lifted imperiously, and her smoky eyes gleamed as she raised her own glass. "And to the lesson I learned. Never trust a man who says he's in love. He can damn well prove his love by taking the risk of marriage with a prenuptial contract that's been cast in iron.''

Wordlessly they each downed a symbolic swallow, and when they had finished, Ariana felt as if somehow they had arrived at a fragile understanding. It was time to go to work.

"My aunt is due to attend another of her psychic's sessions this coming weekend,'' she began in a business-like fashion. "I've already told her I was curious, myself, and wanted to attend. She didn't object when I said I'd be coming up with you; not when I explained that you were someone I've been dating who is also curious. She's quite confident her new guru can withstand a little scrutiny, I guess.''

"Where does this guru live?''

"He has a sort of retreat up in the mountains about a hundred miles from here. Sounds very gothic. Lots of atmosphere, I gather,'' Ariana said dryly as she tasted the salmon. "Anyhow, a small group of people is allowed to attend the séances each weekend. Philomena doesn't seem concerned about getting permission to bring a couple of guests."

"There's a charge for attending?"

"Naturally. A stiff one, too. Actually, I wouldn't be so concerned about the situation if that was all it appeared to be costing my aunt. One expects to pay for any sort of performance, after all. I would assume she'd grow bored with this latest fad after a while and go on to something else."

"But the withdrawals from her account have added up to considerably more than just entrance fees for the sessions?" Lucian hazarded.

"Considerably more," she emphasized.

"What's the name of your aunt's psychic?"

"Fletcher Galen. Mean anything to you?"

Lucian shook his head. "No, I'm afraid not. That doesn't mean much. Probably a, er, stage name."

"You mean an alias!" she scoffed, passing him the salad bowl which he took with alacrity. She suddenly noticed the way he was enjoying the meal she had cooked. Didn't the man ever get home cooking?

"Okay, an alias," he agreed. "Could I have some more salmon, please?" He looked hopefully at the platter.

The discussion continued, but it became increasingly clear that it was the meal which was commanding Lucian Hawk's attention. By the time the walnut torte had been produced he was clearly satisfied with the progress of the evening.

"I warn you I may drag out our working relationship indefinitely if you'll guarantee to keep feeding me," he chuckled as he polished off the torte. "Sure beats eating off of the food stamps!"

"Thank you," she said dryly.

"Don't worry, I know how to pay for my dinner," he told her easily as he helped her carry dishes back into the kitchen.

"You do parlor tricks?"

"How did you guess?"

Ariana set the last of the dishes in the sink and turned to him, wiping her fingers on a hand towel. "All right," she challenged. "Let's see what you can do."

"Are you serious?" he half smiled, eyeing her curiously.

"Why not? I'm hiring a magician, aren't I? I might as well see how good a magician I've got!"

Lucian hesitated. "You're not hiring me, Ariana, remember? This is a partnership."

"Sorry, I'll try to remember," she murmured and reached into a cupboard for two brandy snifters. "Show me your stuff, magician," she commanded, leading the way back to the living room with a bottle of brandy and the glasses.

"Something simple, I think, to start," he said with a trace of amusement as he sat down in the center of the papaya-colored rug. "Got a dollar bill?"

She might as well get into the spirit of the thing, Ariana told herself, locating the required dollar bill in her purse. Then she sat cross-legged in front of him and poured brandy into the two glasses. She assumed he would need a few minutes to arrange whatever little trick he intended to perform, so she occupied herself with pouring out the brandy.

The sound of the dollar bill being torn into shreds brought her head up sharply. "My dollar!" she gasped with the natural chagrin of someone who has a very healthy respect for money. The last of the shredded dollar was just going into Lucian's left hand. "You've just destroyed my money!"

"I thought that would get your attention," Lucian said pleasantly. He showed her the ball of once perfectly good money which was now in the palm of his hand. Then he closed his fingers back into a fist, made a pass or two with his other hand and proceeded to unroll the wad which had been the torn bill.

The dollar bill was again in one piece.

Ariana frowned, her suddenly intent gaze going from the dollar bill to Lucian's topaz eyes. "How did you do that?" she demanded.

"Magic," he reminded her blandly.

"Don't give me that," she ordered impatiently. "How does that trick work?"

"I just told you. Magic."

"Do it again."

Obediently Lucian repeated the trick, tearing the dollar bill into several pieces and then unrolling the ball of fragments to reveal a complete and whole dollar.

Her brows drawn together in a line of unswervable

concentration, Ariana inched a little closer and took a sip of her brandy. "Do it one more time. Slowly."

Lucian smiled and obligingly repeated the sleight-of-hand. Once more Ariana was forced to admit that it looked very much as if her dollar bill had been torn to shreds and then magically made whole. She shifted a little closer on the papaya carpet. Her curiosity was thoroughly aroused now.

"Given your interest in money," Lucian said in low, luring tones, "you might like this little piece of magic, too." He reached into his back pocket and removed a handkerchief and a coin. Then he picked up an empty glass he'd carried in from the kitchen and carelessly rolled up the handkerchief into a small ball which he dropped into the glass. He set the glass with the wadded-up handkerchief onto the carpet between himself and Ariana and then casually made the coin, which had been sitting beside the glass, disappear.

"You palmed the coin!" she accused at once.

"Did I? Look inside the handkerchief," Lucian advised, mouth crooked upward in amusement.

Suspiciously Ariana reached into the glass and pulled out the handkerchief. Out fell the missing coin. She shook her head in annoyance. "Do it again."

"What's the matter, Ariana, don't you believe the evidence of your own eyes?" he mocked, obediently making the coin disappear and then reappear inside the handkerchief.

"Tell me how it's done!" she insisted, moving a couple of inches closer.

Lucian took a sip of his brandy and regarded her speculatively over the edge of the glass. "No," he said finally. "I don't think I will. But I'll give you another chance with another bit of magic. Hold out your hand."

At once Ariana did as instructed. Her frustration was growing by leaps and bounds. With her decidedly practical and intellectual approach to most matters she found it infinitely disturbing not to be able to detect the secrets involved in Lucian's magic. She was determined to catch him in the middle of a piece of sleight-of-hand and find out exactly how he did his tricks.

Carefully Lucian counted out five coins into her palm. Ariana watched with total concentration. "Now count them back into my hand," he instructed in that gentle, come-hither voice. He held out his hand.

Carefully, never so much as blinking, Ariana counted back the five coins.

"We agree there are five coins?" Lucian questioned, watching her avidly alert face with a veiled expression that Ariana ignored. She only wanted to discover how the trick was going to work.

"Agreed."

"Good. Hold out your hand again," he told her and promptly dumped the coins back into her palm, closing her fingers tightly around them. His own hand was clearly empty. "Now watch," he smiled, "while I make one of the coins you're holding so tightly leave your hand and come to mine."

Almost at once he produced a coin from between the fingers of his right hand. Hastily Ariana opened her own closed fist and discovered that she was now holding only four coins. Her patience snapped.

"Damn it, Lucian! Tell me how it's done!"

He smiled tantalizingly, topaz eyes clearly mocking. "I'll give you one more chance to see if you can figure it out."

Once again he began counting coins into her palm. Ariana followed each movement carefully. She couldn't explain, even to herself, why his magic was annoying her so thoroughly. Somehow it had become a matter of paramount importance to expose his secrets. It was as if she wanted to prove to both of them that he was no faster or cleverer than she was.

Deliberately she counted the five coins back into his hand. Whatever he did had to be done at the point where he dropped the coins into her palm and then closed her hand into a fist around them. That must be the moment when the sleight-of-hand took place. She waited, poised to strike.

Lucian saw the tension in her slender body as she sat waiting to pounce. The cool determination in her appealed to him, prompting a sense of amusement and challenge. She was so grimly set on finding out how the magic worked.

But he had been deliberately luring her closer and closer on the plush papaya carpet, because ever since last night he had been wondering what made Ariana Warfield work.

The woman was a mystery to him, and Lucian knew an overwhelming urge to discover what lay behind her cool exterior. What were the secrets hinted at by that unexpectedly soft and vulnerable mouth?

So she wasn't sleeping with Dearborn, the man in the three-hundred-dollar trenchcoat....

He held his hand above hers, ready to back-palm one of the coins so that only four of them would fall into her hand. Ariana waited expectantly, her eyes focused on his palm full of coins. She was going to grab for his hand just as he was concealing one of the coins, Lucian realized with a flash of humor. She was very, very close and when she moved to trap his hand she would be off balance. Which was just the way he wanted her.

Deliberately he started to drop the coins back into her hand.

"Oh, no you don't!" Ariana cried, reaching for his hand with her free fingers.

Lucian didn't argue. He simply encircled her wrist and yanked her gently off balance and onto her back. An instant later she was lying partially trapped under him. He felt her go unnaturally still as she stared up at him wide-eyed.

Very calmly he removed her eyeglasses and then his own. For a timeless moment topaz eyes burned into unreadable smoky blue depths and then Lucian said huskily, ''It's dangerous to interrupt a magician at work.''

Slowly, savoring the heightened awareness of all his senses as his body responded to the woman beneath him, Lucian lowered his mouth to Ariana's.

Three

Ariana's immediate response to the position in which she found herself was astonishment; not that Lucian had decided to kiss her but that she had been concentrating so intently on his magic that she hadn't even been aware of his real goal. The whole magic act, it seemed, had merely been an elaborate diversion, a piece of misdirection. She had been neatly lured into a very old trap.

The knowledge that he had handled her so adroitly was what held Ariana still as Lucian's mouth came down on hers. She simply wasn't accustomed to being so easily maneuvered by a man.

Lucian took full advantage of the moment of astonishment. Holding her wrists firmly but gently pinned to the carpet on either side of her head, he moved his lips with warm deliberation. Ariana felt as if she were being carefully tasted; as if her mouth were being explored to the fullest possible extent. There was a hungry sensuality behind the kiss, and it occurred to her vaguely that she was the subject of his curiosity as well as his desire. Was Lucian Hawk really curious about her?

The realization that he might be searching for some answers about her was disturbing. When his tongue emerged to lightly trace the outline of her lower lip in a coaxing manner, Ariana stirred beneath him.

It was at that point that she had to acknowledge that more than astonishment and surprise was holding her flat on her back on the carpet. Ariana tried to move again and realized that she was physically trapped, as well. Lucian was using the weight of his body and the casual strength in his hands to hold her where he wanted her.

Ariana felt a returning surge of irritation as well as the beginnings of something suspiciously akin to a physical response, and she parted her lips to protest both.

"Lucian, that's enough!..." she whispered more unsteadily than she might have wanted.

But he simply took the opportunity to drive his tongue between her lips, filling the warm interior with such shocking completeness that her protest was cut off before it had really begun.

She felt the accompanying surge of his body as he intimately invaded her mouth, and a small answering tremor went through her slender frame. The effect of her own response was like a tiny dose of electricity passing over the surface of her skin. Every nerve ending seemed to come alive; she was exquisitely aware of a tightening at the nape of her neck and across her midriff, and inside the black ballet slippers her toes curled. Ariana moaned, a small, primitive sound that was half locked in the back of her throat.

Lucian's response was a husky stifled groan that emanated from deep in his chest, and the weight of him seemed to increase. His tongue moved inside her mouth now with a rising urgency, its motion deliberately imitating the far more intimate union to which it was only a prelude. The primitive rhythm seemed to thrill Ariana's senses, freeing them from the bonds of her normal, cool thought processes. Slowly, with ever more complex patterns, they began to whirl.

Magic, she tried to tell herself as her lashes fluttered tightly shut and her hips arched of their own accord into his. He must be using magic on her.

As if the instinctive movement of her thighs were a signal of some sort, Lucian growled her name deeply into her mouth.

"Ariana!" And then his leg moved boldly across hers, sliding aggressively between her knees. He guided one of her hands to the back of his neck, where her garnet-colored nails slid into the black and silver of his hair with trembling expectancy.

The sense of expectancy was as much a shock to her as anything else that had yet happened. Ariana found herself striving to forget about the significance of what was happening. For a few minutes, she told herself, she would sample a bit of what was being offered. The promise of magic had never seemed so tantalizing.

"My God! You feel good lying here under me," he breathed, reluctantly breaking the hot contact with her mouth to trace a silky pattern of kisses along the line of her jaw. "I knew you were going to feel good!"

"Lucian?"

The uncertain, questioning note in her voice ended in a sharp little intake of breath as he nipped gently at her earlobe. Simultaneously his hand came down on her breast. Her body's response was immediate. There was a sudden, aching tautness, and she knew the nipple beneath his palm was hardening. The silk of her jewel-colored blouse and the scrap of lace which was her bra offered little protection. She knew he must be aware of the budding nipple.

His deep growl of anticipation and pleasure was ample evidence that he was satisfied with her reactions. A part of Ariana wanted to retreat; to deny this man the knowledge that he was having such a strong effect on her senses. It was dangerous for a woman to let a man know the extent of his power over her, she reminded herself.

But those words of wisdom were making no impact on her brain tonight. It was easier to listen to the urgings of her senses. Her fingers threaded luxuriously through the darkness of his hair, and she was rewarded with the shudder that coursed through him. His leg moved purposefully along the inside of hers.

His lips were on her throat now, and he arched her head back over his arm, exposing the vulnerable, sensitive curve. When he began to unbutton her blouse Ariana moved restlessly. The danger in his magic was coming closer, and she knew she ought to resist it.

"Oh, Lucian!" The tiny cry came as he unclasped the front fastening of her bra and found the swelling outline of her breast. Instinctively she turned her face into his shoulder, inhaling the warm, male scent of his body.

"So soft," he whispered hoarsely against the skin just above the nipple he was delicately exciting with his thumb. "Soft and gentle and passionate. I was sure there would be something special behind that cool exterior. I had to find out." The words came brokenly, punctuated by small, stinging little kisses that moved closer and closer to their goal until suddenly he had taken the tip of her breast into his warm mouth.

Ariana gasped and clung heedlessly to him, her hands finding pleasure in the thrusting contours of his strong shoulders. "Lucian, Lucian, please! I don't know...I don't think..."

"Hush," he murmured, his voice lulling and deliciously hypnotic. "Hush, Magic Lady. I want to discover all your secrets." He slid his palm down across her stomach, searching out the fastening of the velvet trousers. "By morning I'm going to know exactly how you work."

Morning? Good lord, did he think he was going

to stay the night with her? Awareness jolted through her, sending the magic fleeing. What did she think she was doing letting this near-stranger make love to her! Was she out of her head?

"No. No, Lucian! That's enough. Stop it!" Tremulously and then with gathering conviction Ariana shifted beneath his weight and began pushing at his shoulders.

"Relax, honey," he crooned, voice still hypnotic and full of promise. "Just relax and let me take you where we both want to go."

Ariana sucked in her breath, her head moving in a fierce negative. "Lucian, stop it. I mean it. Let me up!"

He must have heard the underlying element of panic that was seeping into her voice because he stopped his sensual assault and raised his head to gaze down at her intently. She saw the embers of passion that still flickered in the depths of his topaz eyes and held her breath for a tension-filled moment.

What would she do if he didn't release her?

"What's the matter, Magic Lady?" he murmured, gentling her with his fingertips. His mouth curved reassuringly. "Don't you want me? I could feel you responding, honey. Why the panic now?"

"I am not panicking," she retorted angrily. "I'm simply calling a halt to an after-dinner kiss that has gone much too far. I don't know where you got the idea you might be staying until morning, magician, but you're wrong. You're going to pull a quick disappearing act with the assistance of my front door. Let me up, Lucian.''

He didn't move. ''And if I don't?''

''You will.'' She returned his gaze unflinchingly, her voice very steady.

He waited a moment longer and then rolled onto his side, propping himself up on one elbow to watch as she hastily sat up and began arranging her clothing. ''You're right. I will leave. This time.'' The last words came very meaningfully.

''Don't make it sound as if there's going to be a next time!'' Ariana scrabbled on the carpet for her glasses and pushed them onto her nose in a small act of defense.

''You're one heck of a quick-change artist,'' he observed almost casually, reaching for his own glasses and sitting up. ''A minute ago...''

''A minute ago things were getting out of hand!''

''No,'' he countered softly. ''I had everything under control.'' The look in his eyes sent a wave of warmth through her from head to toe.

''You mean you were going to call a halt of your own accord?'' she mocked skeptically as she got to her feet and scooped up the brandy snifters.

''I didn't say that, I merely said I had everything under control.'' He picked up the bottle of brandy and followed her back to the kitchen where he set it on the counter.

''Well, magician, your idea of things being under control varies somewhat from mine, so I think it's time we ended this evening.''

"You're scared of me, aren't you?" he asked wonderingly. "What's the matter? Doesn't Dearborn make you react like that?"

Ariana swung around to face him, cold fury in her eyes. "Let's get something straight, Lucian. I am not in the market for an affair with a magician or anyone else. You and I have a working relationship together and that's all. Stay out of my private life and I'll stay out of yours. Agreed?"

He smiled abruptly, a devastating, wholly masculine smile that was guaranteed to raise the hackles on any woman's neck. Ariana was no exception. "You're quite welcome to invade my private life," he drawled provocatively. "And as long as we're setting the record straight, I'd just like to point out that you were enjoying at least part of that little session on the carpet a few minutes ago!"

Ariana's chin lifted proudly. "I can enjoy an after-dinner kiss as much as anyone!"

"You make it sound like an after-dinner mint!"

"I put it in exactly the same category. A couple are very pleasant. A whole package would be far too much. Good night, Lucian Hawk. I will phone you later this week and let you know the final arrangements for the trip to Fletcher Galen's retreat."

"Would you let me stay if I offered to tell you how to make the coin disappear from the floor and reappear inside the handkerchief?" he tried.

She saw the dawning laughter in his eyes and almost succumbed to it. With firm resolve she managed to keep her face set in unyielding determination.

"You can't bribe me, Lucian. Not by promising to teach me the tricks of your craft."

"What would it take to bribe you?" he asked with a deep curiosity.

"Nothing you have to offer! Good night, Lucian!" Imperiously she went to the front hall closet and hauled out his black jacket.

He took it almost meekly and absently shrugged into it. His eyes never left her face.

"Do you need to call a cab?" she inquired belatedly, feeling unaccountably guilty at the way she was pushing him out the door.

"No. I drove tonight."

"Oh. Well, in that case…"

"In that case there's no excuse for not being on my way, is there?" he finished for her amiably.

The guilt rose a little higher. "Lucian, I'm sorry if I gave you the wrong impression tonight," Ariana said in a contrite little rush. "You're not really angry?"

One black brow climbed above the frames of his glasses, and his mouth curved cryptically as he eyed her. "What's the matter, Ariana? Finally beginning to worry about the consequences of angering a magician?"

That restored her sense of balance very neatly. Ariana flung open her door and wordlessly ushered him out into the foggy night.

"Thank you for dinner, Ariana," he murmured politely and then he was gone.

There was an unnatural trembling in the tips of

Ariana's fingers as she closed the door solidly behind him. Now why in the world should that be? she asked herself uneasily. What was the matter with her? This wasn't the first time a man had tried to take more than she was willing to offer.

But it was the first time in a long while that she had been so tempted to forget all the fine decisions she had made when things had gone so wrong four years ago.

Well, she'd come to her senses and regained control of the situation in time, she reassured herself as she trailed through the living room. She could handle Lucian Hawk.

It was an impulse which made her reach for the phone beside the Queen Anne sofa. Her brother kept very odd hours, and it was a good bet that he was still awake. When he answered cheerfully on the other end of the line Ariana plunged in with the question that was at the top of her list.

"What, exactly, do you know about Lucian Hawk, Drake?"

"What's wrong? Isn't he going to work out?" Drake yawned extravagantly in her ear. "He's a hell of a good magician. A real artist."

"Okay, I'll buy that, but what do you know about him, personally? How did you meet him?"

"Through a friend, a guy who's trying to write a book on Houdini. He knows a lot of magicians. It's all right, Ari. My friend has known him quite a while. He vouched for Hawk. And after I met Lucian

I liked him, too. Don't you?'' Drake added innocently.

Ariana ignored the question. "Is that all you know about him?''

"Well…''

"Well, what, Drake?'' she prodded coolly.

"Lucian and I had a few drinks one night last week and talked a bit.'' Drake sounded more vague than he usually was when he had his mind on a new project.

"And?''

"And nothing really. I gather he's done a lot of varied things. Only to be expected I suppose. I mean, he didn't have a smart sister like you to manage money for him and help him get rich, did he?''

"Drake, if there's something I ought to know before I leave with Lucian Hawk Saturday morning, I'd certainly appreciate it if you would tell me!'' Ariana got out acidly.

"Look, the best I can do is to tell you that the friend who introduced me to Lucian swears he'd trust the man with his life. Furthermore, I, myself, like Hawk. I'd trust him, too. What's the matter with you? Has something happened to make you nervous about the man? I can get some more details from my friend if you want to know them, but I had the impression that Hawk's a relatively quiet person who can be trusted and who knows magic. What more do you want?''

Arian sighed. "Nothing, Drake. He'll have to do. There really isn't time to find anyone else. I've already told Aunt Phil I would be attending the session with her this weekend and that I was bringing someone with me.''

"I still think you're worrying over nothing, Ari. This is just another of Aunt Phil's passing fancies. You know how wild she was about all those films and books claiming that Earth had been visited by alien spacemen thousands of years ago. She always gets excited about the possibility of visitors from outer space. But she'll realize this guy Galen's a phony soon enough.''

"I'm not so sure, Drake. This time there's money involved,'' Ariana stated decisively.

There was a chuckle on the other end of the line. "And when there's money involved Ariana Warfield sits up and takes notice, doesn't she? Good luck, Ari. I'll be anxious to hear the results of this weekend's big exposé. Good night, I've got to get back to this nifty little gadget I'm working on. It's the solution to a single woman's fears in the big city. It looks like a normal lipstick case, but…''

"Good night, Drake,'' Ariana interrupted. She wasn't going to get any more out of him tonight, she told herself wryly. "I'll phone you when I get back from the mountains.''

Lucian Hawk reappeared at Ariana's door precisely on time the following Saturday morning. He got out of the cab carrying a small leather overnight bag and the familiar black jacket. Ariana watched him through the curtains, wondering disgustedly why her pulse had quickened at the sight of the dark-haired magician. She had convinced herself that her body had forgotten the sensuous attack it had undergone on her living room carpet earlier that week.

Now, as Lucian paid off the driver and loped easily up the steps to her front door she was forced to acknowledge that some forms of illogic died harder than others. The sight of him had an uncanny effect on her, and she wasn't sure how to fight it. Remember that you know very little about him, she told herself as she went to answer the door. As if she needed that added bit of caution. Wasn't the fact that he was a professional deceiver enough to make her keep her distance?

"Hello, Lucian, come on in. I'll be ready in just a minute," she said politely, opening the door and stepping aside. He was wearing a pair of faded jeans, a maize-colored oxford cloth shirt and a pair of canvas shoes. Her eyes went over him, assessing his appearance.

"What's the matter? Don't I look acceptable enough to introduce to Aunt Philomena?" he inquired easily, setting down his leather bag.

"I think we can fake it," Ariana said quickly, aware of a red stain on her cheeks. "It's not that you look bad or anything," she tried to explain.

"It's just that I don't look rich?" he hazarded perceptively. He smiled blandly.

"Never mind. You'll do just fine. Everyone dresses casually these days. Aunt Phil won't notice the jeans and shoes, I'm sure!" Hurrying off to the bedroom, Ariana made her escape. What a way to begin the trip! She picked up the shoulder purse lying on the bed and double-checked her own appearance in the mirror.

She was wearing a sassy loden green wrap jacket over a pair of pleated taupe trousers. A crisp yellow tuxedo-style shirt and a pair of elegant glove-leather casual shoes added to the overall effect of easy sophistication. How was she going to look to Philomena when she stood next to Lucian in his jeans? Ariana grimaced to herself and promptly decided to put the issue out of her mind.

She could put the matter of clothing aside but not the underlying problem it had pointed out. "I think we should discuss your background," she announced firmly to Lucian as she emerged from the bedroom.

"I beg your pardon?" He watched her with sudden wariness.

"Not your real background," Ariana assured him hastily. She felt herself flushing again and covered the moment of uneasiness by making a production of collecting her chic yellow cotton duck carryall. "The background we'll have to give Aunt Phil in order to make you sound like a plausible romance possibility. She's going to want to know something about you. Only natural, I suppose. When I told her I was bringing a friend she immediately got excited."

"Has visions of marrying you off, I take it?" he said pleasantly enough, following her outside and waiting while she locked the door.

Ariana glanced at him in surprise and then grinned

wryly as she realized that he had no real knowledge of her unusual relative. "Not at all. You need have no fears on that score! Aunt Phil doesn't really believe in marriage. She thinks a good love affair is far superior to a bad marriage any day. She'd love to see me embroiled in an affair, but I don't think she has any particular wish to see me married. She's never been married herself." Which hadn't stopped Aunt Phil from enjoying more than one discreetly glorious affair of the heart, Ariana thought privately. She headed toward the sleek black Porsche parked at the curb. It was a cloudy, zesty San Francisco day, and the chill of fall hung in the air. "She does know the kind of man I generally date, however."

"And I may have trouble measuring up to the image," he observed dryly. "Your aunt sounds like an interesting woman." He stowed the luggage. "Here, toss me the keys. I'll drive."

"That's all right, I'm used to doing my own driving."

"So am I," he said, pointedly extending his hand.

An imp of mischief came to sit on Ariana's shoulder and she grinned, folding her fingers tightly around the keys. "Why don't you just magically make these keys disappear from my hand and reappear in yours the way you did the coins last night?"

"Okay, watch this," he ordered, grasping her wrist before she realized his intention. An instant later he had pried open her fingers and stolen the keys. "Voilà! Magic! I now have possession of the keys." He held them up with a flourish.

"Some trick!"

"It worked, didn't it? That's all a magician asks of a piece of magic."

Surrendering to the inevitable, Ariana went around to the opposite side and slid into the bucket seat. "About your fictional background," she began repressively as he started the engine and expertly put the thoroughbred car in gear.

"Don't worry, I've got that covered, too," he said easily, his eyes on traffic as he headed for the Golden Gate Bridge. "It occurred to me that your aunt might ask a few questions sometime during the visit."

Ariana shot him a sharp glance. "All right, let's hear it. What sort of background have you decided to give yourself?"

"How about my posing as a reclusive but eminently successful real estate speculator?" he suggested.

"Hmmm. The word 'speculator' is a little sleazy sounding. Let's make it real estate developer and financier," Ariana said thoughtfully, considering the matter closely. "It carries connotations of quiet wealth. I like that."

His mouth crooked wryly. "Because the words 'developer' and 'financier' have a more established ring to them, Ariana?"

"I think so," she said slowly. "'Speculator' has a somewhat here-today-gone-tomorrow sound, don't you think? It smacks of slick dealing and fast maneuvering. Yes, I definitely prefer developer and financier."

"Whatever you say," he agreed neutrally. "As long as it sounds wealthy enough for you."

She heard the mockery in his voice and decided to ignore it. He couldn't possibly understand her fears, and she had no intention of trying to explain them to him.

But what if, Ariana found herself thinking wistfully as they crossed the elegant span of the Golden Gate Bridge, what if Lucian Hawk really did meet her specifications for a husband? Instantly she put a brake on her flight of fancy. That was ridiculous. Even if by some miracle he had money and a spotless reputation, even if he were to fall in love with her, there was still the overriding fact that he had no interest in marriage. He had made that very clear the other night.

She was a fool to even be thinking such wild thoughts, Ariana scolded herself. With a touch of aggression which caused Lucian to slide her a sideways glance, she changed the subject.

The picturesque inn at the edge of the tiny mountain town was charming; quaintly Victorian in architecture. Nestled cozily in the towering pines and fir trees which surrounded it, the place looked as if it had been at home there in the mountains for a hundred years. Aunt Philomena had happily told Ariana that in reality the place had only been built five years previously and that the plumbing, thank God, could be relied upon.

Lucian guided the black Porsche into the small parking lot and glanced around curiously as he switched off the engine. "This is where Fletcher Galen conducts his magic act?"

"The actual retreat is located a few miles from here according to Aunt Phil. People aren't allowed to stay overnight on the grounds. Most of them stay here at this inn. If you do succeed in exposing Galen, the owners of this place probably won't thank you. They're undoubtedly doing quite well on the tourism he inspires!" She opened her door, not waiting for him to perform the small task. "Oh, good. We should be just in time for afternoon tea. Phil will be pleased."

"Tea?" Lucian occupied himself collecting the baggage.

"Umm. Aunt Phil says it's one of the attractions of the inn. That and the late evening sherry hour!" She smiled as they walked into the lobby.

Ariana recognized immediately the apparition standing at the front desk engaged in what could only be politely described as a forceful discussion with the middle-aged clerk on the other side.

Only Philomena Warfield could have pulled off the fashion coup of combining a flowing, flowered caftan, hand-tooled cowboy boots and a brilliantly patterned headscarf wrapped gypsy style around her long silvery hair. And only Aunt Phil would have the audacity to be conducting such an outrageous argument. Ariana felt the heated rush of embarrassment as a blush rose up her throat and stained her cheeks. By now she ought to be accustomed to Philomena's eccentric ways, but there were still times when she could be caught flat-footed and totally embarrassed by them.

"I don't care what you thought I ordered two days ago. I no longer want two rooms for my niece and her friend. I want *one* room. What's the matter with you, man? Are you living in the Dark Ages? This is a modern world we live in and my niece is a very modern woman. Men and women do spend weekends together at places like this, you know! All the time these days! Ariana is thirty years old, and she's entitled to share a room with her male friend!"

"Madam," the clerk began grimly, "the question of your niece's love life is not at issue here. I don't care who your niece sleeps with or where she chooses to spend her nights. What is at issue is the little matter of two guaranteed room reservations. These rooms were held at your request. They could easily have been booked for the evening by other people whom we had to turn away. Now if your niece wants to share a room with her *friend,* that's clearly her business. But someone is going to have to pay for the extra room!"

"That's ridiculous," Philomena declared grandly. "Why should I pay for two rooms when I only require one for her? However, if you're going to be chintzy about the matter, I will pay for both rooms on one condition! You're to tell my niece and her escort when they arrive that there is only the one room available, do you understand?"

Ariana managed to find her tongue. "Aunt Phil!" Caught between the embarrassment of her aunt deliberately trying to arrange a compromising situation and the tall, dark figure of Lucian looming behind her in the lobby with a wickedly amused smile on his face, Ariana could only wish for a genuine act of magic. Something along the lines of having the floor open up to allow her to disappear without a trace. Instead there was only one alternative and that was to get the situation in hand immediately.

"Aunt Phil, you can forget it. It won't work," she grated with what she hoped was cool amusement. There was no hiding her flaming cheeks.

"Ariana, darling!" In a floaty little rush of caftan and perfume Philomena's dainty figure flew across the room to greet her niece. At sixty-two, Philomena Warfield was still a striking woman. Full of energy and talent she lit up any room in which she found herself. "You finally got here! I've been dying to meet your new friend. Drake has been telling me all about him just this morning on the phone. Please don't waste another second. Introduce us, dear!"

Ariana sighed. "Philomena, this is Lucian Hawk. Lucian, my aunt."

Lucian dropped one of the bags he was holding and stepped pointedly around Ariana in order to accept Philomena's delicately held fingers. He inclined his head with a gracious manner which Ariana presumed he had developed in the course of performing before an audience. "I'm very pleased to meet you, Miss Warfield." The words were gravely polite, but the topaz eyes gleamed as he continued, "And I appreciate your efforts on my behalf with the desk clerk.''

Philomena glowed. ''Well, I wouldn't have bothered,'' she confided as they both ignored Ariana, ''if you'd been that Richard Dearborn person Ariana's been seeing so much of lately. But I had a lovely chat with Drake this morning, and he told me all about you. I came to the conclusion that you may be just what Ari needs. In the past four years she's become terribly, terribly cautious about interesting men.''

''I understand,'' Lucian said, nodding.

''Aunt Phil that is enough!'' Ariana interrupted vengefully, wondering what in the world Drake had told her. ''Lucian, stop encouraging my aunt, do you hear me? Both of you are causing me untold humiliation. Just look at all these other people watching us! Aunt Phil, that was a perfectly ridiculous little plot you were concocting with the desk clerk. It wouldn't have worked at all and you should have known it! If Lucian and I had arrived to find only one room, I would have shared yours!''

''Oh, dear.'' Philomena appealed to Lucian. ''She's so unimaginative, isn't she? Well, I did my best. It was worth a try. Come along, both of you, they're just starting to serve tea and I'm sure you could use a cup after that long drive.''

Ariana turned a helpless look on her escort, but Lucian merely smiled kindly and took her arm to guide her in the wake of Philomena.

One thing which could be said about Philomena,

Ariana consoled herself despairingly as her aunt commandeered a table and ordered a sumptuous tea, there was never any lack of conversation in the older woman's vicinity. Philomena kept up a lively monologue while she arranged tea and scones. Most of the discussion was aimed at Lucian, who listened attentively. Ariana could only set her teeth and endure. For his part, Lucian appeared entranced.

"Has Ariana always been so interested in financial matters?" he inquired blandly, oblivious of the seething glance bestowed on him by the lady in question. He lathered butter on a scone and took a satisfyingly large bite as Philomena responded with an indulgent chuckle.

"Oh, my, yes. Since she was in high school. Always seemed to have a talent for handling money, didn't you, Ari?" Before Ariana could answer, Philomena plunged on. "Naturally Drake and I are both extremely grateful, you understand, Lucian."

"You are?" He looked across at Ariana who sat in tense silence.

"Definitely. Drake and I, I'm sorry to admit, would undoubtedly be flat broke today if it weren't for Ari. My nephew and I are both quite talented in our own fields, but we have absolutely no feel for money at all. We simply enjoy spending it. It's Ariana who has invested our earnings over the years for us and built them into comfortable amounts. Drake and I both recognized what an asset she was early on and started turning everything over to her as soon as possible. I don't mind saying she's made us a nice little mint, bless her heart. I do so like having money to spend, don't you?''

"It can be...very convenient," Lucian admitted, still watching Ariana, who was, in turn, focusing totally on the contents of her teacup.

"Everyone likes money." Philomena nodded complacently. "And Ariana is so good to Drake and me. Why, she doesn't even charge us a cent in commission! But she can be awfully proud, too. After that messy business four years ago when she lost everything of her own and was forced to borrow from Drake and me she insisted on paying back every last dollar with interest. We tried to tell her there was absolutely no need but she..."

Ariana turned on her aunt, smoky eyes full of desperate appeal. "No more, Phil," she begged quietly. "Not on that subject. Please."

Philomena was instantly contrite. "I'm sorry, darling, I didn't realize you probably hadn't told Lucian the full story. I should never have reminded you of that awful year."

"Never mind. Just find something else to discuss." Over the rim of her cup Ariana met Lucian's glittering, inquiring eyes. She held that gaze with a steadiness which was belied by the faint trembling in her fingers. She held his gaze, but she didn't like the deep, probing expression she saw there. A wave of uneasy premonition swept over her. But before she could think of anything more to say, Philomena was rushing forward once more.

"No sense rehashing ancient history is there?" the

older woman declared cheerfully as she poured more tea. "The present and the future are the only things that matter, don't you agree, Lucian?"

"Definitely," he stated firmly.

"Well, then, tell me something about yourself, Lucian," she invited brightly. "Drake says you live in San Francisco and that he introduced you to Ari at one of his parties."

"Lucian is in real estate," Ariana said distinctly, wondering why she was bothering to give her escort a respectable cover now. Philomena clearly seemed quite taken with him as it was! "He's a developer. He finances large projects in and around the city."

"Oh, a speculator! How exciting!" Philomena clapped her hands once in appreciation. "I'll bet you're very slick, aren't you, Lucian? Fast and sharp."

Lucian began to laugh. A deep, rich, velvety chuckle that held all the male amusement in the world. Ariana glared at him, but nothing could have quelled that laughter. Philomena stared in puzzled delight, clearly wondering what was so funny, but Lucian was laughing too hard to explain.

Ariana lifted her eyes beseechingly toward heaven, recalling with forceful clarity the conversation she'd had with Lucian in the Porsche about the difference between a speculator and a financier and developer. His sense of humor, it appeared, was as unpredictable and unreliable as that of her aunt's.

"Tell me something," Philomena went on irrepressibly as Lucian managed to control his laughter.

"Has Ari told you about her plan to insist on a pre-nuptial contract in the event that she ever marries?"

"Phil!" Ariana turned once more on her aunt, but Lucian was already answering the question.

"As a matter of fact," he said smoothly, still grinning, "I believe she did mention the subject."

"And what did you think of the idea?" Philomena pressed interestedly.

"I hope I made it very clear that I didn't plan on signing such an agreement," Lucian said flatly, the last of the humor fading from his eyes.

"Excellent," Philomena approved at once. "I've been saying for four years that a man who could convince Ariana to take another chance on love and passion was exactly what she needed. Someone has got to rescue her from this obsession she's developed about protecting herself with contracts and marriage and money! A wild, wonderful affair would do her so much good, don't you think?"

Ariana ran out of fortitude. "I think," she stated grimly, rising to her feet with the royal grace of a queen, "that I'll go to my room and unpack."

She fled the tearoom, leaving it to the magician and the mischievous imp who inhabited it.

Four

Several hours later that evening Ariana sat in a pitch black room, a room so dark that she couldn't even make out the features of the people next to her, and learned that there are situations in this world that are far more unnerving than that of holding one's own with a magician and a wickedly good-natured aunt.

Ariana had never been so uneasy, so primitively alarmed in her life, and the intellectual knowledge that everything she was witnessing was nothing but sophisticated stage magic did nothing to quell the incipient dread.

The lightless room held about twenty other people, including her aunt and Lucian. Philomena knew most of the other attendees at the psychic demonstration and had introduced many of them to Ariana and her escort before the group had been conducted through the high gates of Fletcher Galen's "retreat" and into the massive stone mansion in the center of the grounds.

Galen's assistants had all been sober-faced people dressed in dark, concealing robes that resembled those of a medieval monk. They had said little as they collected the so-called donations at the gate and led people into the darkened chamber where Galen was to make his appearance.

At first Ariana had tried to tell herself that the whole thing was like going to the haunted house at Disneyland, but somehow the seriousness with which everyone took the events made it difficult to keep thinking in those terms. There were, she was learning, some very interesting factors of group psychology involved. When the people around you clearly believed that they were about to witness something wondrous and inexplicable, you found yourself in danger of suspending your own rational thought processes, too.

What Ariana couldn't fully comprehend was why she found herself the most thoroughly frightened person in the room. No one else seemed unduly terrified, merely fascinated and enthralled. Why was she, one of the two people in the room who had come to expose the trickery, so alarmed? Ariana shivered as a faint glow appeared on the small platform in front of the audience. She was suddenly very glad of Lucian's presence beside her.

The glow at the front of the room increased steadily until it revealed a table and a single chair. Ariana didn't care for the eerie, phosphorescent green of the light, but a ripple of anticipation went through the rest of the audience as if it were some sort of signal.

"Relax, will you?" Lucian leaned over to whisper in her ear. "You're the big-time exposer of charlatans and frauds, remember? You're not supposed to lose your nerve at your first séance!"

She could hear the smile in his voice, although she couldn't see his face. With an effort of will she took a grip on herself. Damned if she was going to provide him with another source of amusement tonight. He'd laughed enough at her expense this afternoon.

Before she could think of a snappy response to his bantering, however, a deep, vibrant voice seemed to effortlessly fill the room, and a figure appeared on the stage behind the table and chair. A figure dressed in a shapeless robe of yellow, the front of which was worked with a strange design. There was a hood to the robe, but it was thrown back to reveal the starkly handsome features of a man in his mid-forties. It was a lean, ascetic face, dominated by dark eyes and a strong nose—the face of a man who might have conducted inquisitions in his spare time. The face of a man with a cause. The face of a man who carried a heavy, demanding burden with great dignity.

Fletcher Galen had what was casually referred to as "presence." It was the special gift that made for the finest actors, the most persuasive politicians and the most charismatic public figures. From the moment he entered the room, Galen was the center of attention.

"Good evening, friends," he said. There was a murmur of respectful response. Galen went on in slow, measured tones. "I thank you for coming once more to witness along with me the gentle power of our good friend Krayton." Galen took the chair behind the table.

Ariana shivered and moved restlessly in her seat. On one side Philomena sat expectantly, and on the other side Lucian sat in thoughtful silence, his eyes on the figure in front of them.

"Krayton's abilities to work through me increase daily," Galen announced in a pleasant yet humble tone. "As our mind-to-mind link solidifies and grows strong, so does his ability to channel his other-worldly talent through that link. But as I have explained in the past, your assistance is also a powerful component of these experiments. Through me Krayton can tap your energy and goodwill and use it to conduct the various tests. As with everything else in the universe, all power feeds on energy and energy feeds on power. The two are intertwined and inseparable. Only the nature of the energy changes. Here on earth we have tapped very primitive forms of energy such as fossil fuels and the atom. But Krayton's people have gone far beyond such sources. Tonight you will see just how far they have gone."

Ariana jumped a little as she realized that another person had materialized at the corner of the stage as Galen had been talking. The assistant had his hood up over his face and nothing could be seen of his features as he carried forward a tray of small objects.

"Concentrate with me," Galen intoned as he passed his hand over the tray of objects. "Let Krayton tap into the power of your minds and demonstrate to you the rich resources of the human brain that wait to be set free, just as the resources of his own mind have been set free by the psychic science of his planet. You are the Keepers of the Energy here on Earth."

There followed a demonstration of psychokinesis, the movement of objects by the power of the mind. The assortment of items on the tray alternately floated in midair, snapped in half or disappeared entirely from the room.

It was all accompanied by eerie lighting, the sincere, heavy-toned voice of Galen and the indefinable power of an audience that was only too happy to believe in psychic powers. This was the same crowd who also believed in the Bermuda Triangle and ancient spacemen, Ariana reminded herself periodically. But no matter how frequently she told herself that it was all stage magic, she couldn't control the uneasy reaction of her body and her mind.

The demonstrations grew in complexity until Galen himself floated in midair at one point. Then a member of the audience was put into a trance and declared he could actually see an image of the mysterious Krayton as if he were viewing him through a camera. Philomena leaned over to whisper to Ariana and Lucian that she knew the person in the trance and couldn't wait to talk to him about the experience later.

Gradually the tension and the sense of other-worldliness built in the dark room until almost anything that could have happened would have been blamed on Krayton's psychic intervention. Ariana knew it was all a razzle-dazzle operation, but for the life of her she couldn't fully convince her senses. She sat quietly crouched in her chair, every fiber of her being taut and alarmed. She began to pray that the session would come to a quick close.

And then a soft rush of wind seemed to fill the chamber. Instantly a thrilled silence swept over the crowd, and Fletcher Galen, himself, went absolutely still, as if he, too, was stunned. His dark eyes peered into the space above the heads of the audience, and everyone else's eyes followed.

There was another glowing light, apparently emanating from midair, and in the center of it was the faint outline of an unhuman face.

"Krayton!" The shocked gasp was from Galen. "Krayton, is it possible? Have you actually found the strength to project yourself so far?"

The image in the darkness seemed to turn its head slowly with great effort, and then, as if from across the vast reaches of interstellar space, came a distant voice.

"Not enough. Not yet. Not yet..." The image and the voice began to fade.

Ariana shuddered and felt the last of her rational thoughts desert her. She gasped aloud and groped blindly for Lucian's hand. It closed around her own with instant reassurance, and she turned her head into his shoulder, burying her face in the fabric of his jacket. Immediately his arm came around her in a protective motion that was also somehow very possessive.

But Ariana wasn't concerned with such fine nuances just then. She wanted only to hide from the magic that was fraying her nerves to an extent she would never have believed possible. She was horrified not only by what she had seen but by her own reaction to it!

"Let's get out of here," Lucian ordered abruptly. He leaned over to catch Philomena's attention. "Come on, Phil, I want to take Ariana back to the inn. She's had enough."

"Of course," Phil whispered back, rising immediately to her feet. "But I can't see a foot in front of me!"

"Here, take my hand." Lucian extended his free arm to catch hold of Philomena's wrist. His other arm was still wrapped around Ariana, who was shivering uncontrollably as she crowded close to his warmth.

As she lifted her head from the security of his shoulder another light appeared on the floor at her feet, allowing her to see the carpeted aisle. The addition of yet another inexplicable light made her suck in her breath.

"Flashlight," Lucian whispered dryly. He was holding the pencil-slim object in the hand that was wrapped around Ariana's shoulders, and he used the light to guide his two charges to the curtain through which they had entered earlier. On the other side an assistant in the usual flowing robes hastened to open the door.

"Is the lady all right?" the man asked in solicitous tones.

"She's fine. Just a little nervous," Lucian said blandly, shepherding Ariana and Philomena out of the room and into the wide hall beyond. Without pausing, he led them outside to the lot where Philomena's Mercedes was parked. The keys to the car, which he had driven earlier, appeared in his hand, and in a matter of seconds he had Philomena and Ariana safely inside.

"Ari, dear, are you all right?" Philomena leaned over the seat as Lucian drove back toward the inn. "What's wrong? There was absolutely no danger, you know. Krayton would never harm a soul!"

Ariana shuddered and stared fixedly out the window. It was Lucian who succinctly explained what had happened. "She'll be okay, Phil. Ariana just forgot to make allowances for the power of suggestion on the human mind. Some people are more susceptible than others. It can be a shock to find out you don't have all the control you think you have over your own senses."

Ariana found her voice. "It was magic, wasn't it? All of it. Stage magic." She knew then that she was asking for reassurance. Her voice was a harsh whisper.

"Yes, it was magic," Lucian said quietly. "The man's good and he has a hell of an ability to handle an audience. But it was all stage magic. With a little practice and a skilled lighting technician anyone could have done what he did tonight."

"What!" Philomena swung around to stare at Lucian. "Are you saying it was all trickery?"

"I'm afraid so, Phil. A lot of sleight-of-hand, invisible wires and lighting effects. Nothing unduly complicated." He smiled gently.

"I don't believe you! The man's a direct conduit for Krayton! Everything we saw was an example of Krayton operating through Fletcher Galen!" Philomena exclaimed.

"Phil," he said patiently, glancing at her in the rearview mirror. "I could duplicate any one of the effects you saw tonight and have you believing that you were seeing Krayton in action."

"I'm not saying a good magician couldn't find ways to imitate Krayton's powers, but that doesn't mean that what we saw tonight wasn't real! I've seen it done before, don't forget! I've seen people in the audience go into trances and actually have visions of Krayton's home world!"

"People in a hypnotic trance can be persuaded to have all sorts of interesting visions," Lucian explained quietly. "Look, Phil, let's talk about this in the morning, okay? Ariana's upset enough as it is."

Instantly Philomena was concerned again for her niece. "Ari, dear, listen to me. Krayton is quite harmless. You have no need to fear him or Fletcher Galen. They mean only the best. Don't be alarmed, dear. Goodness, I had no idea this was going to upset you so much!"

"I'm all right, Aunt Phil," Ariana managed huskily, her attention still on the darkened scenery outside the car's window. "Really I am. I just wasn't expecting quite what, uh, happened."

"I know you didn't expect to see such an amazing display of Krayton's abilities," Philomena soothed chattily. "And knowing your practical approach toward life, you probably thought it was all some silly old-fashioned spiritualist séance when I told you about it, didn't you?"

"I just wasn't expecting what happened," Ariana repeated bleakly as Lucian pulled into the inn's parking lot.

"What Ariana needs is a good dose of that sherry I saw sitting on the mantel in the lobby," Lucian announced as he assisted the two women from the car. "I take it it's there for the guests?"

"Oh, yes, help yourself." Philomena nodded quickly. "I think that's an excellent idea. I believe I'll have a little nip, myself."

Lucian seated both women in the cozy Victorian parlor and went to fetch the sherry. They had the place to themselves, since most of the inn's guests were attending Fletcher Galen's séance.

"They'll all be back fairly soon," Philomena explained as Lucian handed her a glass of sherry. "We have the most intensely interesting group discussions afterward."

"I think I'd rather give the discussion a miss if

you don't mind,'' Ariana said as she downed a large swallow of the sherry. "I'm exhausted. I think I'd like to go to bed."

"Of course, I quite understand," Philomena murmured sympathetically.

"I'll take her on upstairs." Lucian poured more sherry into Ariana's glass and helped her to her feet. "If you'll excuse us, Phil?"

Philomena smiled benignly. "Certainly. But don't think this is the end of our little argument, Lucian. Fletcher Galen is not a fake!"

He nodded. "We can discuss it in the morning."

"You don't have to lead me off to bed as if I were a child," Ariana muttered resentfully as he steered her in the direction of the staircase.

"Be careful that you don't spill the sherry," he countered mildly, quite as if she were, indeed, a child.

At the top of the landing she whispered warningly, "If you dare laugh at me over what happened tonight, I swear, I'll steal your magic wand!"

"I'm not laughing at you," he said gently, guiding her to her door.

Ariana took a deep breath as he thrust the key into the lock. Then she took a large swallow of the sherry. "Thank you for getting me out of there, Lucian. I've never been so unnerved in my whole life!" she told him honestly.

"I understand and you're welcome." He closed the door behind them, standing with his back to it as he watched her pace restlessly across the room.

"Well, I don't understand! I knew it was all trickery! Who could possibly believe such drivel?"

"Someone who wants to believe it," he said simply. "And there are a hell of a lot of people who get a charge out of the idea of being visited by alien beings."

"And yet I was the only truly frightened one in the whole room," Ariana whispered, shaking her head dejectedly.

"Some people have a stronger reaction to the power of suggestion than others. You're the kind of person who should never volunteer for a hypnosis experiment, Ariana. I'll bet you were a lot of fun to take on a roller coaster ride or through a haunted mansion at an amusement park," he added with a crooked grin.

She shuddered. "I used to hate both of those forms of entertainment!"

"I can see why. Your head is telling you one thing and your senses another, and the resulting conflict is definitely hard on your nerves. But you were perfectly right, you know. Galen is a first-class fake." He left the door and paced thoughtfully across the room to stand in front of the window. Beyond the glass stretched a darkened vista of pine and fir.

"I thought you were going to stand up and do something dramatic like turn on all the lights and show the invisible wires and the lighting arrangements," Ariana grumbled, flinging herself down on the foot of the bed and kicking off her high-heeled shoes. "What happened to the grand exposé? Houdini made a real name for himself doing that sort of thing, didn't he? Exposing charlatans and frauds who claimed to have connections to the spirit world?''

"Yes." Lucian continued to gaze thoughtfully out the window, his hands shoved into the back pockets of the jeans. "He did."

"I thought you'd see this as your big chance or something," Ariana sighed, taking another sip of the fortifying sherry.

"It wouldn't have been quite that simple, Ariana. I'm sure Galen's smart enough to take protective measures against the possibility of someone in the audience declaring him a fraud and trying to prove it."

"Protective measures?"

"You don't think all those strong young men in the robes and cowls were there purely for atmosphere, do you?" he asked dryly.

Ariana blinked in astonishment. "My goodness, I never thought of that. Do you suppose he hires them to keep the audience in line?"

"I'd say that's probably one of their functions. Anyone who tried to cause real trouble would undoubtedly be escorted rapidly out of the room and thrown off the grounds."

Ariana winced. "How are we ever going to prove anything to Aunt Phil?"

"Your aunt's an intelligent woman, as you have already observed to me. I think she'll see reason." Lucian swung around to face her. "After all, she's smart enough to know that you and I could be very good together,'' he added deliberately.

Ariana's head came up sharply in response to the new tone in his voice. In a flash the uneasiness she had been experiencing since the séance was given another source. It wasn't Galen's magic she needed to fear tonight, it was Lucian's.

''My aunt is an incurable romantic,'' she said firmly. ''Don't get the idea that just because you have her approval you can therefore have me.''

A distant roll of thunder drummed across the night sky.

''There's a storm coming in,'' Lucian said as if she hadn't just issued a challenge.

Ariana smiled a little grimly. ''Thunderstorms are not on the list of things of which I am afraid. I won't be needing any comfort to get through a storm, if that's what you're about to suggest, Lucian.''

''Are you sure?'' he drawled gently. He was watching her the way she imagined a sorcerer watched a magic pentagram, waiting to see what would appear in the center. The fateful sense of premonition that she had experienced briefly during tea swept over her again.

Irritably Ariana got to her feet, shrugging off the prickle of awareness and the strange, intoxicating fear that accompanied it. She could feel those topaz eyes on her, sensed the waiting quality in him and she wanted to hide, just as she had wanted to hide from the other kind of magic earlier in the evening.

But somehow Lucian's brand of magic was far

more threatening. "I think it's time you left," she ordered huskily, meeting his gaze in the mirror over the dressing table. "Good night, Lucian."

He said nothing but moved slowly to stand directly behind her, watching her in the mirror. She could feel the desire in him and with a shock felt the answering flicker of sensual tension that sprang to life in her veins. His jeweled eyes held hers with invisible bonds as he stood behind her.

"Do you really want me to go, Ariana?"

She swallowed and unconsciously steadied herself by holding onto the edge of the dressing table. "Yes." She didn't think she could move. What would she do if he reached out and took hold of her?

"I want you," he whispered and then his hand moved to stroke the line of her shoulder. "Badly."

Wordlessly Ariana shook her head, trying to stifle the shiver that coursed through her at his touch. What was it about this man that tantalized her so? Why did it have to be Lucian Hawk of all people who could have this effect on her?

"Just tell me that you know how much I want you," he murmured persuasively. "Tell me you are aware of the attraction between us."

"Lucian, there's no point..." she began urgently.

"Tell me and I'll leave," he interrupted coaxingly. "I want to hear you say the words."

"Why?" she got out starkly.

"Because there's magic in the words." He half smiled, dropping the most delicate of kisses into her cinnamon hair. "Didn't you know that? And the magic is strongest when you say the words aloud. Tell me you know how I'm feeling." The tips of his fingers moved again on the curve of her shoulder and Ariana quivered.

"I...I know that you want me," she said and instantly regretted having spoken. He was right. Saying the words aloud gave them some kind of power. It was as if by having voiced them herself, she had in some fashion acknowledged his *right* to want her. "But *I* don't want you, Lucian," she grated fiercely, turning to face him. "I do not want an affair with you! How many times do I have to say it?"

"Until you've convinced yourself, I suppose," he said politely. "Good night, Ariana. I'll be right next door if you decide after all that you're scared of thunderstorms." He bent and kissed her lightly, lingeringly, as if casting a tiny spell on her mouth, and then he turned and left.

There was a crackle of electricity in the night time sky as the door closed behind him, and Ariana was left wondering why there was power in his words but none in her own.

With an effort she shook off the effects of his presence and doggedly went about the process of getting ready for bed. Too much had happened this afternoon and this evening, she consoled herself as she undressed and slipped into a lacy peach-colored nightgown. It was no wonder she was feeling overwrought.

Overwrought. Now there was a fine old Victorian expression suitable for use in an inn such as this!

She glanced wryly around at the hotel room, which had been done as an excellent reproduction of a romantic, old-fashioned lady's bedroom. The wide bed came complete with four carved posts and a thick lace-trimmed quilt. The furniture was heavy and solid, and there was a charming flower print on the wallpaper.

As she climbed up onto the high bed, Ariana decided that she understood now why ladies of the past century occasionally gave way to a fit of the vapors. There were times when no other reaction would quite do! Leaning across the quilt, she turned out the bedside lamp and idly watched the gathering storm outside her window. It was going to be a violent one from the looks of things.

It seemed perfectly suited to the events of the evening, she thought with a sigh. Memories of the séance drifted back into her head, and she knew a surge of anger at Fletcher Galen for having shown her the weakness in herself. The man deserved to be exposed!

The rain began then, pounding fiercely against the sliding glass doors that opened onto her balcony and had been patterned to resemble French windows. She lay on her side, watching the light and crackle of the thunderstorm, and thought about Lucian Hawk.

What right did he have to want her? What right did he have to force her to acknowledge that wanting? And why had she been so weak as to admit it at his command?

There were a lot of "whys" and "ifs" going

through Ariana's head, but the most treacherous question of all was why did it have to be Lucian Hawk who left her mind and body tantalized and aware?

He was wrong for her. All wrong.

Slowly her lashes closed as sleep came to claim her and quiet her churning thoughts. There was a lot to talk over in the morning, not the least of which was how they were to go about convincing Aunt Philomena that she was involved with a fraud.

In the morning she would be stronger, Ariana told herself just before she drifted off to sleep. Her normal will and common sense would reassert themselves after the shock they had undergone at the séance. Stupid, being so easily frightened like that. Very stupid. Thank goodness Lucian had realized how upset she was and had taken steps to get her out of that damn chamber.

And in her dreams it was that sense of Lucian's reassuring presence that seemed to hold sway that night. The element of magic seemed irrevocably bound up with the reassurance and protection. It didn't make any sense, really, because what Lucian offered was unstable, unreassuring and dangerous.

Outside, the storm continued gathering its forces, streaking the sky with lightning and rumbling through the air with thunder. Curled in the middle of the fourposter bed, Ariana dreamed of a dark-haired magician who wanted to claim power over her.

And because he was so interwoven in the fabric of her dreams, Ariana knew only a sense of inevitability when her lashes fluttered open two hours later in response to a particularly loud crash of thunder. There on the balcony, silhouetted by a burst of lightning, stood her magician.

Ariana stared at the night-shrouded shape of him, unable to move as Lucian calmly opened her sliding glass door and stepped into the bedroom. He was a man of midnight and shadow as he crossed slowly to her bed.

And when he stood at last looking down at her tense, still figure, Ariana knew that the magic he wielded tonight was strong enough to suspend the future and all her logic.

Five

It was a night for magicians to be abroad.

Behind Lucian the wind howled and light flashed in the black sky. It was a night that belonged to the elements and to the man who could wield their power.

Ariana watched the magician by her bed and knew that for her this man commanded that power. The attraction between them was unlike anything she had ever known before, and even though her logic dictated the safe path of avoidance, this was not a night for logic.

Above her the topaz eyes were pools of ancient mystery and unshielded masculine desire. Lucian towered over the bed for a long, lingering moment, drinking in the sight of her, and then his voice came, soft and deeply intent.

"Ariana, I want you tonight."

He reached down to touch her tangled hair and then he was shrugging out of the black jacket, letting it slip unheeded to the floor. Underneath he wore only his jeans.

It seemed to take all the energy in the world just to say his name in gentle question. "Lucian?"

"Come and take a chance with me, Magic Lady," he whispered, sitting down heavily on the edge of the bed and leaning over her. He trapped her body with his hands and stared down into her heavy-lidded eyes. The dark-framed eyeglasses had been left behind in his room, and without the shield of the lenses his gaze seemed to gleam with honey-colored fire. Ariana stirred and knew her pulse was quickening rapidly.

"I'm afraid of you, Lucian."

"You aren't afraid of me," he countered. "You're wary of me and cautious, perhaps, but you're not afraid of me. By morning you'll know all you need to know about me." He lowered his head slowly. "And I'll know all I need to know about you."

His mouth closed over her parted lips, allowing the combined warmth of their bodies to intermingle at that one point. Otherwise he didn't touch her, although she sensed the weight of him poised just above her breasts. The kiss was a slow, hungry, luxurious caress meant to be a prelude to the banquet from which Lucian wanted to feast. His lips slipped damply across hers, persuasive and full of promise.

How could anyone be afraid of this kind of magic?

Ariana asked herself as she moaned beneath the touch of his lips. This was the kind of sorcery a woman could search for and never find during the whole course of her life. A thrilling quiver of desire raced through her, tightening an invisible coil in her lower body.

"Yes, Lucian. *Yes,*" she breathed on a sigh of passionate surrender.

He groaned huskily against her mouth. "You won't regret it, Magic Lady. I swear I'll take care of everything."

She didn't understand his words, but there was no chance to ask for an explanation. In a swift, wrenching movement that spoke volumes about the level of his own urgent desire, Lucian pulled himself away from her and unfastened his jeans. In a moment he stood perfectly nude, perfectly male beside the bed.

She thought that he would come to her then, but instead he seemed to be waiting. Ariana looked up at him and tried to read the taut, harsh lines of his face. Then she took hold of the edge of the covers and tugged them aside, her eyes never leaving his.

The invitation was as eloquent as it was ancient, and Lucian accepted it with a rasping exclamation. "Ariana!" He slipped into bed beside her, gathering her in his arms and pressing her onto her back.

Ariana's hands came up to first touch and then cling to the curves of his smoothly muscled shoulders. The strength in him was a source of excitement, conveying both a physical and a mental power that appealed on several levels. She tested his skin with the tips of her nails as he began to explore her mouth with his tongue.

The violence of the storm was a fitting backdrop for the storm of passion that Lucian began to unleash. His tongue surged again and again between her lips, demanding a response from the sensitive interior of her mouth that she could not have withheld even had she wanted to do so. Her own tongue emerged hungrily to involve itself in a passionate little duel that ended on the inside of his mouth. Once there, Ariana's desire seemed to escalate more and more rapidly as she tasted the essence of him.

He let her revel in the experience, parting his lips willingly and encouraging her with husky little groans and little nips with the edges of his teeth.

And while she lost herself in the thrilling discovery of her own power, Lucian slid his hands along the line of her throat to her shoulders, seeking the lacy straps of the peach-colored nightgown. The garment was lowered to her waist before she realized what had happened, and by then it no longer mattered.

"Oh, Lucian!" Ariana's mouth broke free from his long enough to gasp his name as his palm cupped her breast with a possessiveness that should have startled her but didn't in that moment. *"Lucian!"*

"Can you feel the tightness here?" he growled hoarsely as his thumb grazed one aching nipple. "Can you feel the way it's becoming tight and hard for me? And the softness here," he breathed, caressing the underside of her breast. "My God, Ariana, you are going to make me lose my head tonight, do you know that?''

He touched each nipple again, circling them with thumb and forefinger and tugging slowly so that Ariana cried out softly in passion and nipped at his shoulder. With lingering, teasing movements of his hands and lips Lucian built the tension between them until Ariana began to writhe beneath him. When he took her fingers and placed them against his thigh she responded willingly, touching him with intimate gentleness. "Ariana, Ariana," he whispered again and again as she slipped her fingertips along the thrusting hardness of him. "Touch me all over, sweetheart. All over!"

Quivering under the force of her own desire, Ariana sought to obey, longing now to please as much as she was being pleased. Her hands moved with soft wonder, learning the flatness of his stomach, the feel of the muscular, male buttocks and the driving power of his manhood.

In turn Lucian was lost in a tantalizing exploration of her soft, exquisitely feminine body. His lips closed over one nipple as his hand passed over her hip and around to the inside of her thigh. Ariana trembled and he soothed her with his low, hypnotic, deeply sensual voice. "Tonight you're going to take a chance with me, sweetheart. There's no other way. Tonight we'll both take a leap in the dark. Open yourself for me, darling. Let me touch you the way I need to touch you."

Over and over the husky words were crooned in

her ear until the magic of his voice was as much a caress as the feel of his hands. Ariana's nails dug passionately into his thigh as she obeyed the lulling, encouraging commands and parted her legs.

"Ah, sweetheart!" He sought the silk of her, threading his fingers through the tangled thatch of dark, cinnamon brown hair. Ariana sucked in her breath as he inevitably found the ultrasensitive heart of her passion. She turned her face into his shoulder, clinging to him as she had clung earlier that evening when fear had been the impetus.

And as it had on the first occasion, Lucian's arm closed around her with fierce possessiveness as he held her close and teased the center of feminine sensation. It flowered for him, revealing mysteries and a need that was as strong as his own. The flowing warmth was a heady, exhilarating call to his senses.

Ariana's lashes closed tightly against her cheeks as she gave herself up to the moment and the man. "Please, Lucian. Please come to me. I need you so," she whispered in a throaty tone filled with unchecked wonder. Never had she known a need so strong that it caused her to plead for a man's fulfillment. But never had she been under the spell of magic before, either.

"I want you so badly, Magic Lady." He loomed over her, broad shoulders blocking out the shimmer of lightning in the sky behind him. For an instant the golden brown jewels of his eyes burned over her face, and then Ariana shut her eyes once more, unable to endure the intensity of his gaze.

Slowly, with infinite masculine power he brought his body to hers, his rough legs sliding aggressively between her soft thighs, the crisp, curling hair of his chest enveloping the berry-hard peaks of her nipples, his mouth taking hers in absolute possession.

Ariana felt him ready himself for the final union. It was as if he were gathering her completely to him. Then his hips surged strongly against her, and he filled her slowly and totally.

Lucian's breath caught in his throat as the impact of the physical bonding washed over him. He felt its reverberations going through the soft frame of the woman under him and knew he was not alone in sharing the sensation. She was right for him, so very *right!*

Burying his head in the curve of her shoulder, he held her with near-violence and began to build the magic rhythm that would bring them both the secrets of the universe. He knew an utterly primitive, utterly glorious satisfaction at the evidence of her response. It was essential that she find pleasure in his arms. He had to begin staking a claim somewhere, and this was the most basic method of all for doing so. The need to satisfy her thoroughly, to wipe out the memories of any other man she had ever known was a powerful goad to all his senses.

The biting pain of her nails in his shoulders, the tightening pressure of her soft legs around his hips and the little gasps which came from her lips were sources of infinite gratification. Lucian's body and mind were both thoroughly caught up in the turmoil of passion and need. The words he whispered against her throat were dark and heavy with an elemental excitement. He reveled in her response to them. He reveled in *all* her responses.

At last he felt the fragile tightening of her body beneath his and knew that she was on the brink of the ultimate physical sensation. His own body reacted fiercely to the knowledge and threatened to overwhelm what little was left of his self-control. With ferocious willpower he kept his senses in check. It was essential that she be satisfied first. He had to know that she had given herself completely at least on this level.

"Lucian! *Lucian?*"

He caught his name as it left her lips and heard the uncertainty in it, the hint of panic. "Take the chance, Magic Lady. You have no choice. Take the chance!"

He slid his hand below her tenderly rounded derriere and arched her tightly against his hips, his fingers clenching deeply. It was enough to send her into the final, delicate convulsion.

"Oh, my God, my God!" The low moan was half-stifled in her throat as every fiber of her body tightened and then went into shimmering release.

Lucian felt the roaring exultation in his veins and surrendered to the mindless climax at last. He had made her his, irrevocably his.

Ariana came languidly out of the pleasant haze of the aftermath, aware first of the weight of Lucian's body which still sprawled across hers in magnificent abandon. No, in magnificent possession.

The second realization came quickly on the heels of the first, and Ariana stirred with a faint unease. There was a sense of complete and total possession in the way the magician lay along her body, his head on her breast, his hands somehow having caught hold of her wrists. The heaviness of his thighs trapped her legs.

Ariana felt a return of the incipient panic that had blossomed just before she had surrendered completely to Lucian's lovemaking. Firmly she squelched it. There was no cause for panic. She was a mature adult, a woman with needs that had been too long held in check.

But even four years ago when she had thought herself so wildly, blindly in love, the need and the desire hadn't been like this.

Nothing had ever been like this.

And that thought brought back the hint of panic. After so many years of being so very, very careful how did she come to find herself in this situation? In bed with a magician, a man who was totally at odds with every one of the requirements she had set down for a husband. *A man who didn't even have any intention of becoming a husband!*

"What is it, Ariana?" Lucian lifted his head, and she knew that he must have felt the tremor that had gone through her. His eyes smiled down at her, warm and tender but with an underlying expression of lazy victory that couldn't be masked. His mouth crooked with indulgence and remembered pleasure, and he lifted a hand to stroke back a strand of hair that lay along her cheek. "Are you starting to worry already?"

Her lashes shifted as she looked up at him with clear honesty. "I always worry when I take chances."

"You won't have cause to regret taking this one, honey," he drawled reassuringly.

"Won't I?"

"No. I can give you what you want. But I had to know that you would surrender first without demanding financial statements from the banks and an iron-clad contract. I was a little afraid to take a chance, myself," he added with a wicked little smile. "But now we've started off on the right foot. Everything's going to be okay."

She stared up at him in confusion. "What are you talking about, Lucian?"

"Forget it. I'll explain everything in the morning. Right now all I want to do is enjoy what's left of the night. Magicians always do their best work at night, you know."

He leaned down to kiss her, and the toe of his foot moved excitingly along the calf of her leg. Ariana felt the faint stirrings of renewed passion and wondered at it.

Magic. It was the only explanation. She let her arms circle his neck once more and pushed aside the confusion and doubts that had begun to assail her....

* * *

In the morning both the storm and the magician were gone.

Ariana stirred and woke, instinctively feeling for the warmth of the man who had lain beside her during the night. When she found only the empty bed next to her she sat up groggily, blinking away the last traces of sleep.

There was still an indentation on the pillow where Lucian's head had rested, and when she buried her nose in the down-filled thickness of it she thought that she could detect a hint of the unique and satisfying scent that was his alone.

What was the matter with her, sitting there amid the sheets and inhaling Lucian's fragrance from a pillow? Tossing it aside, Ariana tried to bounce lightly off the high Victorian-style bed and nearly stumbled as her body proved unexpectedly sore in various places.

She drew in her breath in surprise. Her body was rather forcibly reminding her of the solid strength of the man who had spent the night with her. Holding onto the bedpost, Ariana stretched, working out the voluptuous aches in her muscles. Lucian had been a demanding lover, but he had repaid her for the response he had taken with a seemingly inexhaustible masculine passion.

When had he left? Continuing on her way to the bathroom, Ariana frowned as she tried to figure out what would happen next between them. Obviously he had gone back to his own room sometime near dawn. There had been no further chance to talk.

What did a woman say to a man over breakfast the next morning after a night such as the one that had just passed?

Ariana felt restless and confused as the shower water cascaded down around her. Last night Lucian had refused to deal with the crisis he had created, using sensual magic to take her mind off the subject of their future whenever she would have tried to return to it.

She didn't have the impression he was ignoring that future, only that as far as he was concerned, it was settled and there was no real need to discuss it. He had promised to explain everything in the morning.

What did that mean? What was there to explain? The restlessness and confusion grew as her thoughts became more chaotic. She could hardly believe that she had been so cautious for so long only to wind up giving herself in a blaze of desire to a man who wasn't at all what he should be. That thought kept clanging around in her brain, occasionally colliding with a memory of that same man's tenderness or a recollection of his concern for her during the séance. Images of the startling, overpowering figure he had made silhouetted against the storm as he walked into her bedroom also intruded, sending little frissons along her nerves.

The night had belonged to the storm and the magician who was a part of it. What of the day?

Deciding that her only defense against the unknown lay in such familiar feminine tactics as choosing clothes that would enhance her self-confidence, Ariana walked back out of the bathroom and carefully dressed for the trauma of breakfast.

She belted a shawl-collared long-sleeved blouse in a foulard print over a slim yoked skirt that fell to her calves. Then she added a pair of soft suede high-heeled boots. The overall effect was sophisticated and dashing. Just the impression she wanted. Sophistication and dash could cover up a multitude of uncertainties and vulnerabilities, she told herself as she picked up her hotel room key and started for the door.

The realization that she had been safely locked in her room last night swept over her just as she put her hand on the doorknob. Hesitantly she turned to glance at the sliding glass door through which Lucian had entered. She could have sworn that door had been locked before they had left for the séance. Which meant that he must have deliberately unlocked it before he had left her room the first time last night. She remembered how he had been standing near the window with his back to her, and she remembered how good he was at sleight-of-hand. Lucian had known full well that he would be returning when he had said good night to her that first time.

A little dazed at the sheer audacity of the man, Ariana continued downstairs. Aunt Phil would be waiting to have breakfast with her in the inn's dining room.

As soon as she walked through the double doors of the charmingly decorated room she saw that her aunt was not alone. Seated at the table across from her was Lucian, his dark hair, jeans and black pull-over sweater making him a strong note against the white linen of the breakfast room. He looked up almost at once, as if sensing her arrival, and then he was on his feet, coming toward her with a satisfied smile and a look of anticipation in his eyes.

"Good morning, Ariana," he murmured huskily, bending down to brush the lightest of husbandly kisses against her mouth before taking her arm and leading her back to the table.

Husbandly? No, that was definitely the wrong word, Ariana reminded herself firmly as she greeted her aunt. Philomena looked rather like a large bright-eyed tropical bird this morning, dressed as she was in the colors of exotic plumage, which somehow flowed together quite perfectly.

"Good morning, dear. Feeling recovered from your bit of shock last night?"

Ariana reached for her coffee cup, and her eyes collided with the topaz ones across the table. She firmly resisted the urge to inquire which shock her aunt meant. The shock of the séance had, after all, only been the prelude to the evening!

"I'm fine, Aunt Phil. Sorry I made you leave early last night. I hope you didn't miss anything important," she muttered, diligently searching the bread basket beside her and discovering a warm scone.

"No, no, not a thing. The session ended soon after we left, according to my friends. Poor Krayton was unable to get through, but we are all vastly encouraged by how much was accomplished this time,'' Philomena said cheerily.

Ariana bit her lip. ''Aunt Phil,'' she began sternly, striving to find the right words to squelch her aunt's cheerful belief in the quackery of Fletcher Galen.

''Never mind, Ariana,'' Lucian interrupted quietly. ''Your aunt and I have come to an agreement.''

Ariana looked up in surprise, frowning. ''What sort of agreement?''

''I'm going to check into Galen's background a bit further, and if I find out anything Phil ought to know, I'll tell her. Fair enough.''

Ariana opened her mouth to say something about the money involved, but the warning expression in Lucian's eyes made her close it again. She subsided in annoyance and buttered her scone.

''I'm quite sure Lucian won't find out anything bad about Mr. Galen,'' Philomena assured her chattily. ''But I've agreed to keep an open mind.''

''Well, that's something, at least,'' Ariana sighed.

''Lucian also tells me you'll be leaving early today for the drive back to the city,'' Phil continued. ''Lovely day for a drive, isn't it? That storm certainly caused a fuss last night, but it made everything so bright and fresh this morning, didn't it? Did the storm bother you on top of the session with Krayton, Ari, dear?''

''I managed to get through it all right,'' Ariana said dryly, not looking at Lucian.

''Good.'' Phil smiled and nodded. ''I was afraid

it might have added a bit too much *atmosphere* to the evening for you!''

It was Lucian who injected the last comment. ''I, for one, found it contributed to a very memorable evening.'' White teeth gleamed in a laughing masculine grin that made Ariana seriously consider inserting the tines of her fork into his hand. With an effort of will, she resisted.

An hour later, Lucian had packed their bags back into the Porsche and said his good-byes to Philomena Warfield. ''Take care, Phil. I enjoyed meeting you and I look forward to seeing you again soon.''

''Enjoy the rest of your stay here at the inn,'' Ariana said a little hesitantly as she kissed her aunt good-bye. ''You'll be here for a week?''

''Yes, Fletcher Galen has passed the word that we came very close to a major breakthrough with Krayton last night. As long as the energy level is running so high he feels we should all take advantage of it. There are going to be several intense attempts to make direct contact this week. So exciting!''

''Yes, well, uh, good luck,'' Ariana said weakly as Lucian wrapped an arm around her shoulders and began steering her toward the Porsche. ''Call me as soon as you get back to the city!''

''Oh, I will!'' Philomena watched Lucian bundle her niece into the front of the Porsche and smiled grandly. The older woman looked quite pleased with herself, Ariana decided uncomfortably. Or pleased with Lucian.

''Why are we rushing off so quickly?'' Ariana demanded as Lucian slammed the car door and started the engine.

"Because we have things to do back in the city and we've done all we can do for the moment here," he explained as if she weren't too bright.

"You mean you're going to start checking out Galen today? On Sunday? Won't all the agencies you'd have to contact be closed?"

"Galen can wait until tomorrow." He glanced at her with a small smile edging his mouth as he guided the Porsche out onto the main road. "You and I have other things to accomplish today."

"Such as?" she asked, hearing quite clearly the slightly waspish tone in her own voice. Ariana's sense of unease and her innate wariness had not been dispelled. She felt uncertain and far too vulnerable beside this man.

"Such as clearing up one or two matters between ourselves."

"Oh. I see." She looked at him blankly, not knowing what else to say.

Lucian grinned and put a hand on her knee in casual affection. "I doubt it, but you soon will."

"I wish you wouldn't try to be mysterious this morning," she complained, massaging her temples. "I'm really not up to it."

He squeezed her knee. "You did look somewhat beleaguered when you appeared in the dining room doorway this morning. I'm sorry, sweetheart, I've been a little rough on you, but that's because I'm not accustomed to taking chances, either. At least, not the kind we were taking last night.''

''What are you talking about, Lucian?''

''I'm talking about the way we were both trying to circle the other at a wary distance until we knew for sure what we wanted. It could have gone on indefinitely, you know, and my nerves weren't up to that! That's why I forced the issue last night.''

''Are you trying to tell me the logic behind your decision to…to come to my room last night?'' she asked carefully, gazing directly ahead of her through the windshield.

''I suppose so. I couldn't figure you out, Ariana. On the one hand you seemed like such a mercenary little witch,'' he chuckled wryly. ''I wanted to take you across my knee and paddle you the first night I met you. Even your relatives freely admitted you wouldn't look at a man who didn't meet your financial specifications. It was infuriating!''

''A woman has a right to limit the risks she takes,'' Ariana said woodenly.

''Maybe,'' he agreed surprisingly, ''but I didn't want you to apply those standards to me and find me lacking. I wanted you to want me the same way I wanted you. And I kept telling myself that there was a lot more to you than met the eye. Your brother and Philomena both seem to adore you. I sensed a softness and a vulnerability in you just below the surface and I wanted to tear away the facade and find it.''

''Lucian,'' she began anxiously, not at all sure where this was leading.

"I'm not very fond of mercenary women, and you're not very fond of men who don't have bank accounts that match your own. We were at an impasse, honey, and I decided one of us was going to have to take a chance." He shot her an apologetic sideways glance. "Last night seemed like a good time to get the initial clash of arms over with."

"You mean you decided I could be the one to take the chance," she clarified dryly.

"I'm afraid so," he agreed regretfully. "I wanted to know you'd come to me willingly even though I didn't meet your financial requirements. And you did," he concluded with deep satisfaction. "You surrendered so beautifully, sweetheart. I'm going to remember last night as long as I live, do you realize that?"

The panic began to swim like a shark in her stomach. "And what am I supposed to remember?" she managed bleakly. "That I let myself be pushed into taking a chance on a man who doesn't believe in commitments?"

He swung his head around in a quick movement, astonishment plain in his expression. "I know how to make commitments, Ariana. And I know what I expect in return."

"An affair?"

"Most definitely an affair," he growled, downshifting for one of the many curves in the mountain road. "We still have a lot to learn about each other, Ariana, but we know enough already to realize that what we feel for each other is special; full of potential. I'm not one for wasting that kind of potential, are you?''

Ariana felt the shark of panic swim a little closer to reality. ''I...I need time to think, Lucian.''

His hands tightened fractionally on the wheel. ''Now that the basic decision has been made we'll take it easy,'' he promised quietly. ''I want you to get to know me better and I want to get to know you. But like it or not, the affair began last night, sweetheart, and there's no going back for either of us.''

The feeling of inevitability which she had known when she'd opened her eyes the night before and had seen him waiting at her window returned. It was true that all Lucian wanted was an affair and she had promised herself never to take that kind of chance again. Yet a part of her was urging her to do exactly that: To take a chance on an affair with this man.

They would take it easy, he said, get to know each other. Perhaps, just perhaps, there really was something special here, something she should take the risk of discovering. Last night had been unlike anything she had ever known. Did she really want to walk away from such warmth and passion?

It was true that Lucian was a far cry from what she had promised herself she would look for in a man, but Drake and Philomena both liked him. She no longer fully trusted her own emotional reactions, but she'd never had any cause to doubt theirs. They were good judges of character.

My God, she thought, sitting deeply into her seat as she watched the mountain scenery. What was she doing? Trying to rationalize her own desires? Probably. She was on the brink of throwing away all her long-held requirements for a man, even the requirement of a marriage with a contract. For it was unlikely that there'd be any kind of marriage at all with Lucian Hawk.

The churning of her inner thoughts kept her silent for most of the return trip to San Francisco. Lucian didn't try to push her into conversation, apparently lost in his own considerations. It wasn't until after they'd crossed the bridge and had begun heading for an affluent section of the city that was some distance from her own neighborhood that Ariana finally realized that something was wrong.

"Lucian, where are we going?"

"Home."

"Your home?" She didn't want that, she realized. It was too soon.

"Ummm. I want to show you something." He smiled, looking quietly pleased with himself.

"Show me what? Lucian, what are you up to now?" she demanded suspiciously.

"I only want to prove that there are rewards for women like you who take chances on men like me," he drawled as they climbed one of the city's most quietly elegant hills.

"Rewards!" Genuine alarm filtered through now.

"Ariana, last night I asked you to give yourself to me without any strings attached. I know that put you in a vulnerable position. Today I'm going to make it up to you."

He turned the Porsche into the underground garage of a handsome condominium building which overlooked the Bay. Without a word he parked the car and helped her out, ignoring her taut, questioning glance. In silence they rode the plushly carpeted elevator to one of the top floors, and in silence Lucian led Ariana down the hall to a heavy oak door.

Then he inserted a key in the lock and pushed the door open to reveal a brilliant vista of San Francisco Bay as seen from the living room of an expensive, beautifully decorated condominium. Ariana simply stood on the threshold of the elegant room, staring at the expanse of windows ahead of her.

"Welcome home, Magic lady," Lucian said quietly from behind her.

She whirled around to face him. "This is your home?"

He nodded, watching her expectantly. "When it comes to money, sweetheart, I could buy and sell you a couple of times over. Does that reassure you about the chance you took last night? You've made it clear that you want a man whose income level at least matches your own. Well, I'm more than able to do that."

"Why didn't you tell me?" she managed tightly, a cold fury beginning to build inside her as she stared up at him.

"Because I wanted you to take the chance of giving yourself to me first," he admitted calmly as if it were the most natural thing in the world that she should be the one to take the risks.

"You deceived me," Ariana whispered. "You created an illusion and let me believe in it."

"You jumped to conclusions and chose to believe in that illusion," he countered a little roughly, topaz eyes narrowing.

"You could have straightened me out at any time!"

"I could have, but I wanted to make you mine first," he said deliberately.

Her rage soared higher as she confronted him with sudden fierceness. "My God, magician, did you think this would miraculously make everything all right?" she grated, waving a hand to encompass the richness around her. "Did you think you could play the rich king in the fairytale who dresses as a pauper and then sets out to win the princess?"

"Ariana," he began firmly, clearly beginning to perceive that something had gone awry with his plans. "Listen to me."

"Listen to you! That's what I did last night! That's what I've been doing all along. I've been listening to you spin a web of illusion and deception, and now you expect me to tell you it's all right? Did you think that like the princess in the fairytale, I was willing to take you for what you pretended to be, but I'd be thrilled to find out you're actually rich and that we're all going to live happily ever after? Well, you'd better think again, magician," Ariana declared furiously. "I might have been willing to accept the fact that you didn't meet my financial requirements, but *there's no way in hell that I will ever accept the fact that you deceived me!''*

''Damn it, Ariana!'' He moved, intending to block her path, but Ariana was too quick. She snatched the Porsche keys from his hand before he realized her intention.

And then she fled down the hall to the waiting elevator as if all the magicians in the universe were after her.

Six

Ariana made the phone call to her brother as soon as she walked into her apartment. Flinging down her carry-all, she crossed the papaya-colored carpet to pick up the white phone beside the sofa. Drake Warfield sounded rather vague on the other end of the line, and she knew that she'd caught him in the middle of some serious bout of thinking. Ruthlessly Ariana fought to get his full attention.

"You heard me, Drake, I said what exactly do you know about Lucian Hawk?"

"Ari, you asked me that question a few days ago, and I told you that I liked the guy and had heard he could be trusted. What more do you want to know? What the hell happened up there in the mountains, anyway? You sound a little upset."

"Upset is an extremely mild word for what I'm

feeling! And don't you dare tell me you don't know much about Lucian! I think you knew a lot more than you told me a few days ago!''

There was a thoughtful pause on the other end, and Ariana could practically hear her very intelligent brother putting two and two together. ''I take it you found out he's more than just a magician?'' Drake finally asked carefully.

''Oh, yes, Drake,'' she bit out furiously, ''I found out. This morning. But you and Aunt Philomena knew all along, didn't you?''

''Well, I knew he wasn't exactly a pauper, Ari, and I did mention to Aunt Phil when I talked to her Saturday morning that he seemed perfect for you…''

''Perfect for me! *Perfect for me?*'' In the face of such brotherly audacity she couldn't find a suitable response. Ariana felt stunned. ''Why the hell didn't you tell me he was rich?''

''Now, Ari, he's not super rich, just wealthier than you are,'' Drake temporized. ''But what's the matter with that? I thought you'd be pleased!''

''So did he!'' she grated. ''But you didn't answer my question, Drake. Why didn't you tell me? Why did you allow me to believe he was just a magician?''

''He is a magician. A damn good one.''

''Drake!''

''Okay, okay, Ari. I didn't tell you because he asked me not to,'' Drake said simply.

Ariana went momentarily silent in the face of that response. ''I see,'' she finally managed icily.

"Ari, it's not as bad as it sounds," Drake said, trying to placate her. "After we were introduced by our mutual friend, I told Lucian why you wanted a magician and he sounded very interested. He was curious about you. We, uh, had a few drinks and I told him how cautious you are about men. How you wouldn't consider dating someone without money...."

"For God's sake!"

"Now, Ari, it's true," Drake pointed out gently with brotherly forthrightness. "You've been vetting your dates on the basis of their financial statements for the past four years and you know it."

"That's my business, Drake!"

"At any rate, we kept talking about you, and I told him you were really very nice except for this hangup you seem to have developed about men who don't have as much money as you do."

"Did you tell him what happened four years ago, Drake?" Ariana demanded.

Drake sounded shocked. "Of course not, Ari! I would never tell anyone about that! But you're letting it ruin your whole life and I think it's time you started being realistic. Anyone can get conned, and while I'll admit it's not very pleasant, you shouldn't judge everyone else you meet on the basis of what a con artist did to you!"

"Forget it, Drake. You just don't understand," Ariana interrupted bleakly, lowering her forehead into her hand and massaging it. "Just finish telling me what happened between you and Lucian."

"Nothing much beyond that. As I said, over a couple of drinks I told him why you needed a magician and that you tended to be a little prejudiced about men, but that basically you were okay. Hell, I can't remember everything I said, Ari. You know how it is when a couple of men start sharing a few drinks!"

"No, I don't know how it is, but I'm beginning to get an idea!"

"Now, calm down. That's really all there was to it. He said he was interested in meeting you and discussing the job you had in mind, but he asked me not to say anything about his main line of work. I think he's in real estate or something," Drake added as if struggling to remember the conversation. "I like him, Ari. On Saturday morning I phoned Aunt Phil and told her you were going to arrive with someone who was a nice change of pace from Dearborn. She asked a lot of questions that I more or less had to answer. After all, I didn't want to talk about the fact that he was also a magician and that his main reason for going with you was to check out her psychic. It seemed safer to talk about Lucian's background, or what I knew of it."

"And what, precisely, do you know about his background, Drake?" Ariana snapped. "What else did you learn about him while the two of you were having that lovely man-to-man chat and getting drunk?"

Drake sighed. "Just that he's made his money in real estate and that he seems to have come up the hard way. I think maybe he was in and out of trouble a lot as a kid. Not much of a family life from what I could gather. Parents split up or something and more or less let him fend for himself. I don't think there was much money. Anyhow, he ran away from a foster home where he'd been stashed one year when he'd gotten too wild for his mother to deal with. I think he told me he lied about his age and got a job with a traveling carnival. I guess that's when his hobby of magic began to come in handy.''

"My God," Ariana groaned weakly. "A carnival magician. A natural con man."

"Now, Ari, that's not fair," Drake told her grimly. "How do we know what we would have been doing if we found ourselves in his shoes? You and I were just damn lucky there was someone like Aunt Phil to look after us!"

"Never mind. Anything else, Drake? Any other little tidbits you might want to tell your trusting sister?" she whispered scathingly.

"No, that's about it, except that I like and trust him. I honestly thought he might be good for you. When he asked me not to say anything about his financial status I agreed. Now it's your turn, Ari. What happened up there in the mountains?"

Ariana closed her eyes and thought of the storm that had taken place outside her window and inside her bedroom. Then she said very steadily. "Galen's a fraud, of course. Lucian says he could duplicate any of the stunts that were used in the séance. Aunt Phil is having too much fun thinking she's helping to make contact with someone from another planet, though. She doesn't want to hear about Galen being a charlatan.''

"So what happens next?" Drake persisted.

"Aunt Phil apparently agreed to listen to Lucian if he could supply her with some proof that Fletcher Galen's a con man. Ironic, isn't it? I wanted a magician to catch a magician and I got something even better. I got a con artist to catch another con artist. Except that my *partnership* with my con man/magician more or less terminated this morning, so I may have to find another con man. No, that's not necessary, is it? I already know Fletcher Galen is a crook, so maybe my next working relationship should be with a private detective! I'm meeting such an interesting crowd of men lately, Drake!''

"Ari, you sound bitter," Drake began worriedly. "You've told me what happened as far as Galen's concerned, but what happened between you and Hawk?''

"Exactly what you and Hawk planned to have happen," she flung back fiercely. "I was deceived, conned, misled and generally made a fool of. Rather like I was four years ago.''

"Ari! What the hell are you talking about? Lucian wasn't after your money!''

"No," she agreed. "I'll grant you that much.''

"Then why do you say he made a fool of you? Just because he didn't bother to present you with a financial statement?" Drake demanded. Then he seemed to finish putting the pieces of the puzzle together in his mind. "Wait a minute, I get it. You started falling for him, didn't you? That's why you're so furious this afternoon. You're mad because he misled you for a while about his true status and you're piqued.''

"You don't understand, Drake. You never did understand," Ariana repeated, suddenly very tired. "But never mind. It doesn't matter. I'll talk to you tomorrow." She hung up the phone and leaned her head back against the French vanilla sofa cushion.

It wasn't really Drake's fault for not understanding. Ariana admitted as much to herself. She had never told either her aunt or her brother the full extent of her involvement with Marsh Sutcliff four years ago. Oh, they knew about the financial aspects of the situation and they knew that she had been dating Sutcliff, but they never realized that it wasn't a simple swindle he had conducted. Ariana had trusted him with all her money because she had loved him to distraction. She would have done almost anything for Marsh Sutcliff.

Almost, but not quite. Somehow she had managed to draw the line at turning over Drake's and Philomena's money to him along with her own.

The phone beside her rang imperiously, and Ariana automatically reached out to pick up the receiver. "Yes?" It would be Drake calling back.

But it wasn't Drake. "Ariana, I want to talk to you," Lucian said bluntly.

"That's going to be tough, because I don't want to talk to you," she whispered.

"Have lunch with me tomorrow. You'll have

calmed down a little by then and we can sort this out.''

''No.'' She hung up the phone again and unplugged it from the wall.

That night before she went to bed Ariana doublechecked all the locks on her doors and windows. There was no trusting a magician.

The next day she sought refuge in the pleasant, businesslike hum of activity at the downtown offices of Warfield & Co., Financial Planners. It was not a large business in terms of employees, but it was a highly successful one, and the offices of its president had been decorated by Philomena Warfield to reflect that success.

Ariana sat in a padded leather chair behind an ultramodern glass-topped desk and deliberately lost herself in her work. There was a soothing quality about the paneled walls, which had been hung with works of abstract art that Philomena had produced. The paintings had already appreciated three times since she had signed them and hung them in Ariana's offices. A Japanese kimono stand displayed a brilliantly designed ceremonial robe on one wall, and the white carpet, which ran from wall to wall, set off the black leather furniture and glass fixtures.

With a diligence that had built her success twice from scratch, Ariana applied herself to the reports in front of her. The coffee cup at her elbow was never empty, and she had lost track of the number of cups she'd had since arriving at the office at seven-thirty that morning. Too many, she was sure. She was beginning to notice a fine trembling in the tips of her fingers. Well, at lunchtime she would eat something solid. Perhaps that would mitigate some of the effects of the caffeine. On the other hand, she needed the caffeine to offset the effects of a restless night. It was a vicious circle.

It was twelve o'clock when her secretary buzzed her from the outer office. Ariana had just been staring morosely at the coffee cup, wondering whether or not to refill it one more time before lunch when the discreet interruption came.

"Yes, Beth?"

"There's a Mr. Lucian Hawk to see you, Miss Warfield," Beth Dexter's voice said briskly. Beth only called her Miss Warfield when she was conveying strong disapproval of the visitor in question. Lucian must have created a stir in the outer office, Ariana decided grimly.

"Tell him I'm busy, Beth." Lucian would be able to overhear that on the speaker that sat on Beth's desk. She made no effort to soften the crisp executive sound of her voice. Ariana used, in fact, the same tone of voice she used when she was trying to avoid a salesman. There was instant silence as Beth cut off the connection. Ariana realized that she was holding her breath and watching the closed door of her office as if there were several dozen cobras on the other side. Hadn't she read somewhere that one of Houdini's greatest tricks had been the art of walking through walls?

She didn't have to wait long. Lucian didn't literally walk through the door. He simply flung it open and strode across the white carpet to stand before her desk. Then he leaned over, planting his palms on the glass surface, and pinned her to the chair with a glittering gaze.

"I came to take you to lunch."

Ariana's fingers clenched into the padded arms of her chair as she glared back at him. "I'm not interested in going to lunch with you. I thought I made that clear last night. Please leave my office at once."

Even as she spoke a part of her was noticing the transformation in his appearance. Until now she had only seen him in casual clothing that could have been worn by almost anyone at any point on the economic scale. Today Lucian Hawk had effected another piece of magic. He had transformed himself into the essence of the powerful corporate executive. His black and silver hair was brushed to perfect obedience. His vested chalk-stripe wool suit was tailored with an assertive, conservative hand to define his lean waist and broad shoulders. His button-down shirt was subtly striped to complement the suit, and his tie was silk, Ariana decided, or she'd eat the silk blouse she, herself, was wearing under her own white suit.

"We're having lunch together, Ariana," Lucian announced evenly, every line in his harsh face etched with masculine assertiveness.

Ariana swallowed uncomfortably and refused to back down. "No."

"You won't leave the office with me?"

"Absolutely not!"

Lucian didn't move except to lift one hand off the glass and snap his fingers in the direction of the doorway behind him. His eyes never left Ariana's as a figure pushing a wheeled table appeared on the threshold.

"What in the world?..." Ariana broke the glaring contest to stare at the scene taking place in her office. The man pushing the cart was dressed in a black and white waiter's outfit, and the cart was set with white linen, silver and china. A display of food could be seen under the glass dome cover. Without glancing at Ariana, the waiter began setting up the meal.

"Magic, Ariana," Lucian explained dryly. "You won't come out to lunch, so I have no choice but to make lunch appear here in your office."

"Lucian, you can't do this!" she stormed. "Tell that man to take that cart away this instant!"

"Do you really think I'm going to do that after going to all the trouble of arranging the trick?" he growled sardonically.

Helplessly Ariana watched as the waiter finished arranging the repast to his own satisfaction and then, with a formal bow in her direction, left the office, shutting the door behind him.

"First we'll have a little of this very excellent Monterey County Pinot Blanc," Lucian decreed, stepping to the cart and hauling a bottle of wine out of the silver chiller. "And then we'll get down to business." He poured out two glasses and handed one to Ariana with a flourish. "To the future," he intoned, downing a healthy swallow.

Ariana reached for the wineglass, not because she intended to drink to his toast but because just then she needed something to settle her jangled nerves. Silently she sipped the wine as Lucian surveyed the linen-draped cart.

"Shrimp and scallops in pastry shells, mushroom and celery salad and a ham mousse with peach chutney. Shortcake for dessert or fruit and cheese. Which will you have to start, Ariana?"

The sensation of utter helplessness in the face of unpredictable behavior kept Ariana in her seat. "The salad and the seafood, I think," she heard herself say very distantly. He served her with a style worthy of the tuxedo-clad waiter.

"I've waited a few tables in my time," he explained easily as she watched him.

"Was that before or after you did the carny circuit?" she shot back coolly.

One black brow arched behind his glasses. "I see you've been talking to your brother." He drew up a chair across from her and sat down to enjoy his meal. "What else did he tell you about me?"

"That you were in and out of trouble a lot as a kid, that you ran away to join a carnival and that you are currently in real estate. You really are a speculator, I take it?"

"Financier and developer," he corrected smoothly, biting into a sourdough roll. "Remember?"

"Speculator," she asserted cuttingly and focused on her shrimp and scallop dish.

"Words," he said. "It amounts to the same thing in terms of success. I don't need your money, Ariana. Have you settled down enough today to at least admit that I'm not a financial threat to you?"

"How do I know what kind of a threat you might be? You've deceived me once, why not again?"

His face hardened. "Ariana, you have a way with insults that is going to land you in trouble one of these days."

"More threats about the dangers of angering a magician?" she tossed back in icy tones. "Don't bother. I'm not interested in hearing them."

He eyed her, the fingers of one hand drumming lightly on the surface of the table. "Just remember that you've been warned."

"Thanks. I'll keep it in mind!"

He clearly made a grab for his patience. "Ariana, are you really so angry just because I didn't tell you the truth about my financial status?"

Her head came up abruptly. "Funny you should ask that. My brother asked me very much the same thing. What's the matter with you men? Can't you understand?"

"I could understand your being a little annoyed," he said calmly. "But in the end what does it matter, honey? You were willing to accept me in your bed, to take a chance on me, when you thought I was merely an itinerant magician. I can't believe you have lost all interest just because I turned out to fit your financial requirements!"

"You don't understand!" she exploded furiously. "You just don't understand!"

"So tell me," he growled. "What is it I don't understand? Ariana, I'm not after your precious money. I've got enough of my own. Furthermore, you and I are more than compatible in several areas," he added meaningfully. "It's true I'm not interested in signing a marriage contract with you, but since I'm not a threat to your financial empire, what the hell does that matter? You don't have to protect yourself from me, so there's no need for the prenuptial agreement."

"Is that an offer of marriage *without* an agreement?" she inquired far too sweetly and had the satisfaction of seeing his eyes narrow.

"I've told you from the beginning that I'm not interested in marriage," Lucian said quietly.

"Oh, yes, that's right, I almost forgot. You want a woman to take a *chance* on you, don't you? You want her to take all the risks."

"What risks?" he grated. "You don't need my money any more than I need yours. You're not taking any financial risks by having an affair with me, and the only other risk I asked you to take was Saturday night when I came to your bed. That particular risk is behind us now. You took a chance then, I'll admit, giving yourself to a man who apparently didn't meet your monetary requirements. But you were willing to overlook that little matter Saturday night. Why the hell are you so upset, now that you've found out it never was a genuine risk in the first place?"

Ariana lost her temper. The strain on her nerves had become too great to ignore the provocation of his words. She flung herself out of the leather chair and stood facing him with the air of a small cornered animal that no longer has any option but to lash out in self-defense.

"I'll tell you why I'm so angry, Lucian Hawk," she breathed in a ragged tone. "I'm angry because while it's true you managed to meet one of my requirements in a man, you failed miserably to satisfy the other one, which I have always considered even more important. You lied to me, Lucian. Not only that, but your whole background suggests that you've made deceit an integral part of your lifestyle. Just what sort of trouble were you in when you were a kid?"

He hesitated. "That was a long time ago, Ariana."

"Tell me!"

He leaned back in his chair, watching her warily. "I ran with a gang of boys for a while. It was a little rough, but where I grew up it was the logical social organization. Just ask any social worker," he murmured blandly. "I seem to recall talking to a number of them up until I was sixteen."

"And after that?" she persisted, her mouth dry as she pictured him wearing leather and carrying chains and knives. A gang member. Probably its leader, she thought savagely.

He shrugged, his eyes never leaving hers. "After that I joined a carnival. I was the chief magician." Lucian's mouth turned down wryly. "I was also the guy who repaired the equipment, settled squabbles between townies and carnies when they arose, rigged the arcades so that the paying customers didn't win too often, you name it. After that came the army and Southeast Asia. After that came a decision that it was better to be rich than poor.''

"And how did you carry out that decision, Lucian?'' she questioned starkly.

"The same way you did. With a lot of hard work.''

"Hard work and a little slick maneuvering?'' she persisted.

"Slick maneuvering, as you call it, is the name of the game in real estate, honey,'' he informed her bluntly. "That's why I laughed so hard the other morning when you were trying to draw lines between speculators and financiers. There aren't any lines.''

"And how about the lines between legal and illegal?''

"Those are a little vague at times, too, Ariana,'' he told her stonily.

"Are you telling me you've crossed them on occasion?''

His fingers tightened around the stem of the wineglass as he raised it to his lips. Something dangerous showed in the depths of his eyes. An angered magician, Ariana thought fleetingly. "I don't think I'm going to tell you anything else until I find out what this is all about,'' Lucian stated coldly. "Why the inquisition?''

"Because you've lied to me once, and I just

wanted some idea of how long a history you have of deceiving people," she flung back. "Apparently you've been walking pretty close to the edge for a long, long time." She leaned forward, planting her own palms on the glass top of her desk very much the way he had done earlier. She spaced each word out very carefully. "Not only do I make it a point to avoid men whose financial backgrounds don't match my own, Lucian Hawk. I also avoid men whose reputations won't stand the light of day. I am looking for a man of honor, something you'll probably never understand. I might have been willing to bend the first requirement, but I will never again bend the second!"

She saw the cold fury in him, but she also saw that he had it under control. The knowledge wasn't particularly reassuring. Somehow the control he was exerting over his anger seemed to make him all the more dangerous. "Meaning you bent that rule once before?" he rasped softly.

"I made that rule along with the one about finances four years ago, Lucian," she gritted.

He was suddenly on his feet across from her. "Tell me about it!" he commanded even more softly.

Ariana couldn't stop herself. She had gone too far now. "His name, or rather, one of his names, was Marsh Sutcliff. He was handsome, charming and sophisticated. I fell in love with him. I trusted him. I gave him a tremendous amount of money to invest. *And after that I never saw him again.*"

He waited, as if knowing there would be more.

Ariana drew in her breath. "After he disappeared, leaving me financially devastated, I learned that Marsh Sutcliff was a professional con artist. Under a variety of names he'd run scams all over the country. The one he'd run on me had been one of the easiest of his career, apparently. I was in love with him, or thought I was. It was like taking candy from a baby for him, I'm sure," she concluded in disgust. "If I'd done a little serious checking on him, I would have learned that his past was murky, to say the least. But I didn't. The law finally caught up to him somewhere in Florida where he was running a land fraud scheme. But I was a fool and it cost me."

"How much did it cost you?" he asked brutally.

"My money, my heart and all of my pride!" she tossed back savagely.

He glanced around the office. "You've rebuilt the financial end, and I learned Saturday night that you're not breaking your heart over some other man. You couldn't have given yourself to me the way you did if there was another man who held the key to your love. So that leaves us with your pride, doesn't it? That's the one point that is still vulnerable, isn't it, Ariana? You've recovered from everything else but not the humiliation of knowing you'd fallen for a con man. That's why you made those rules of yours. To protect yourself from ever making the same mistake again. To protect yourself from that kind of humiliation!"

"I congratulate you on your powers of perception, magician!"

"So now you think that I'm another Sutcliff?" he asked in a voice of steel.

Ariana flinched at the direct question. That was what she'd implied, wasn't it? "I took the risk of bending one rule for you, Lucian, and look where it got me. In bed with a man who doesn't worry overmuch about a little deception when it's in his own interests. You deceived me. You have to admit that your actions don't speak very well for your sense of honor. At least I was never anything but honest with you, Lucian!"

His hard mouth tightened. "No," he agreed roughly. "You were always honest. You were also bigoted, prejudiced and snobbish. There was also the very real possibility that you were exceedingly mercenary. Hell, woman, can't you see that I was as nervous about you as you say you are about me?"

"I won't take any more risks for you, Lucian!"

He swore, a short, graphic oath that made Ariana step back a pace. "Oh, yes, you will, Ariana Warfield. You bent one rule for me on Saturday night. I can promise you that sooner or later you're going to bend the second rule for me, too! You're going to accept me, murky past and all! You're going to take me as I am, ex-gang leader, ex-carny-showman, ex-G.I. and full-time sleazy real-estate speculator and magician. And you're going to admit that I have a sense of honor, after all!"

"Why the hell should I do that?" she yelped furiously. "Damn it, magician, why should I take one more risk for you?"

"You haven't got any choice," he gritted. "You belong to me. You've belonged to me since Saturday night and probably before that if I wanted to start dissecting the relationship."

"That's not true!"

"It is true," he countered quietly. "But if it makes you feel any better, you have the satisfaction of knowing this relationship works both ways. I belong to you just as surely as you belong to me."

He moved then, his hand making a slight, graceful motion in midair, and then he extended his palm, uncurling his fingers to display a single yellow rosebud on a stem.

Ariana stared at it in consternation as he laid it gently on the glass in front of her. "Good-bye, Ariana. Thank you for lunch. And, honey, try to remember all those warnings about the dangers of getting a magician angry. Don't do anything you'll regret."

She tore her gaze away from the small rose and lifted it back to his face, her own features a study in mingled astonishment, chagrin and anger.

But Lucian was already at the door and through it before she could summon the words to tell him that he had no place in her life and never would. Slowly, the wind leaving the sails of her temper, Ariana sat down at her desk. Unable to stop herself she reached out and touched the rosebud with the tips of her fingers. Trust Lucian to have the last word and the last trick up his sleeve.

Dear God, what was she going to do now? Lucian

Hawk would have no qualms about using whatever means necessary to achieve his goals. Any man who had run with a teenage gang, worked the carny circuit and scraped together a successful real estate empire probably knew a hell of a lot more about getting what he wanted than she did.

Ariana shivered and stared at the rose.

He wanted her.

What really made matters difficult was the frightening knowledge that she wanted him. With a shaky sigh, Ariana forced herself to admit the truth. What she felt for Lucian Hawk was more than desire. Simple physical attraction she could have dealt with, Ariana was certain. This strange emotion that had begun plaguing her was far more insidious; far more potentially dangerous.

Her hand folded shut around the rose and, holding it in her lap, she swiveled around in the leather chair to stare out the sixth story window of her office.

Why couldn't Lucian have been perfect? Why couldn't he have fit her image of an honorable man the way Richard Dearborn did? Why couldn't Lucian have arrived in her life complete with a spotless reputation and a sense of personal integrity that couldn't be doubted? Why couldn't Lucian Hawk have been safe?

Ariana blinked as she recognized the paradox of her own thoughts. The truth was, she *didn't* doubt Lucian's personal integrity. A man or a woman was the product of his or her experiences. To wish that

Lucian's background was different was to wish that he was a different man altogether.

And she could not imagine herself with a different man now. It was Lucian Hawk, the product of a checkered past and a business career that probably used as much sleight-of-hand as did his hobby of deception, with whom she was in danger of falling in love.

Seven

The flourish with the rose had come out all wrong. He'd meant to give it to her with a kiss, not a threat.

Lucian's mouth turned down in self-disgust, and the hand that had produced the rose twenty minutes earlier balled into a large fist. He was standing at his office window gazing with unseeing eyes at the sailboats on the Bay.

It wasn't only the bit with the rose that had gone awry. Everything was going wrong! Damn it to hell! He ought to have realized that it wasn't just her concern with money that stood in the way. She was far more vulnerable than he'd guessed. After what had happened to her, it was no wonder she insisted on complete honesty in a man.

With classic masculine arrogance he'd thought the discovery of his true financial status would remove any doubts that she might still have been harboring. After all, she'd already taken the risk of giving herself to him. Finding out that there was no need to worry about his being impoverished ought to have been the grand finale to the sleight-of-hand act he'd been carrying out since meeting her. But instead of amazing and delighting his intended audience, the magic revelation at the end had precipitated disaster. Lucian groaned feelingly and turned away from the window. He threw himself into the chair behind his desk and stared broodingly at the final subdivision report for the condominium development he was supposed to be considering.

He couldn't focus on business today. All he could think about was the magic lady who was trying to disappear from his life. He couldn't let her go. Lucian knew that with chilling clarity. The well-developed instincts that had brought him so far from the streets of Los Angeles were screaming at him to reach out and grasp this woman. He didn't try to put a label on his emotions. Lucian only knew that he wanted Ariana Warfield.

Why in hell hadn't he realized that with a woman like her things were going to be a lot more complicated than just resolving the financial problem? He'd thought he could simply pull that particular rabbit out of the hat and she would move in with him! What a fool he'd been.

The money had only been part of it. Rule number one, as she'd called it, and he'd managed to make her break it. But rule number two left him with no defense. He'd have had to be one hell of a magician to pull off the impossible feat of making his actions over the past few days disappear! Why hadn't he seen the potential trap he'd been setting for himself when, out of a curiosity he couldn't even explain at the time, he'd decided to keep silent about his personal background the night he'd met Ariana?

Face it. He'd out-finessed himself. A fine magician! But if there was one thing he'd learned in the past thirty-nine years, it was that a man couldn't afford to look back. The only route out of a dilemma was to keep plowing forward, using whatever tools came to hand.

Deliberately Lucian forced himself to cool down and think logically. Ariana was angry now; hurt. But that was something to which he could cling, wasn't it? Better by far to have her feeling some intense emotion toward him than nothing at all. Everything would have been hopeless if she'd simply dismissed him from her life with casual, disgusted indifference.

The drawback to having a passionate woman like Ariana in this particular mood was that it might impel her to do something rash; to lash out recklessly at him. She was woman enough to sense instinctively that her greatest weapon would be another man. Lucian's stomach knotted as he thought of Richard in the three-hundred-dollar trenchcoat. And that image, of course, was what had prompted him to throw out the warning along with the rose.

It should have been a kiss. He knew that he could make her respond to his kisses. Why the hell had he succumbed to his territorial instincts and delivered a threat, instead?

With a wrench he dragged his raging thoughts away from that fruitless path. Logic was what was needed now. Coolly he examined the alternatives available to him. Then he leaned forward and stabbed the button on the intercom.

"Mrs. Kingsley, get hold of that private investigator we used last summer on the Morrison project. Tell him I want to see him this afternoon."

"Yes, Mr. Hawk. Shall I tell him what the conference will be in reference to?"

"A con artist named Fletcher Galen."

Lucian released the button and sat back in his chair, steepling his fingers. He eyed the glass paperweight on his desk as if it were a crystal ball. The strongest tie he had to his magic lady right now was the tenuous partnership they had originally agreed upon. She was probably already thinking of it as dissolved, but Lucian told himself that he would use every trick he had up his sleeve, and helping her prove Galen a fraud was the single most elaborate one he had available. He had to let her know that he still considered the business partnership active. Once again he leaned forward and stabbed the intercom button.

"Yes, Mr. Hawk?"

"Mrs. Kingsley, after you've contacted the investigative service, I want you to call a florist and put in an order for six yellow roses to be delivered here this afternoon."

Mrs. Kingsley had been working for the man who was part magician, part real estate entrepreneur for over five years. She'd learned to expect the unexpected. Her proper secretarial tone didn't alter by so much as a nuance as she acknowledged the unusual request.

But safely out of sight in the outer office Elvira Kingsley allowed a small satisfied smile to brighten her pleasant middle-aged features. It was about time Lucian Hawk found someone for whom he cared enough to order yellow roses on company time. Mrs. Kingsley realized that Hawk had a social life but never had it been permitted to encroach on business hours. Now, in the course of one day she had been obliged to order a catered lunch for two, and a half-dozen yellow roses. Hawk had arrived back from the luncheon with the most deliciously forbidding expression on his hard face. And now the roses. Things were becoming interesting, she thought as she reached for the phone.

The first of the yellow roses greeted Ariana when she opened her apartment door the following morning. She had been running late after a restless night and was feeling irritated with herself and with life in general when she threw open the door and nearly ran into the rose.

It wasn't lying on the mat, it was floating in midair at eye level.

After her initial start of surprise, she realized that only one person would have arranged to deliver flowers in such a fashion. Cautiously she extended a hand to clasp the levitated rose and found it attached to an almost invisible nylon string that was, in turn, suspended from the top of the doorway. There was a tiny card dangling from the rose stem.

Knowing that Lucian had been so close gave Ariana an unexpected sense of excitement which lightened momentarily the depression that had been plaguing her. He had been there sometime during the night, standing right outside her door! What would she have done if he'd knocked?

Hastily she tore down the rose and opened the small note. The inside read merely: *I'll get Galen for you.* It was signed with a handsomely scrawled "L."

Ariana's fingers trembled ever so slightly as she stared at the note. She was aware of both a sense of disappointment over the fact that the note was almost businesslike and a conflicting sense of relief that Hawk intended to carry out his end of the partnership.

The business between them would make it necessary for her to see him again.

The ambivalent feelings she experienced at that thought were chasing each other about in her head as she walked to the black Porsche parked at the curb and turned the key in the lock. The yellow rose waiting inside the car on the dash made her draw in her breath.

There was no note attached this time, but Ariana acknowledged to herself that the placement of this flower was a little trickier than the first. Her car had been locked all night, and there was no sign that it had been tampered with.

But it was the rose waiting for her in her office chair that elicited an unwilling admiration for the sheer audacity of the man who had placed it there. The highrise office building that housed Warfield & Co. along with several other businesses was well patrolled at night. Lucian would have had to get past the guard and at least two locked doors. Unless, of course, Ariana reminded herself with a strange little smile, the man really could make roses materialize behind locked doors.

The fourth rose was waiting for her on a stack of letters that Beth brought in for her to sign that morning.

"Don't ask me how it got there," the secretary said, grinning. "I went to pick them up and bring them in to you and there it was!"

The fifth rose was waiting for Ariana on the seat of the Porsche when she left work that evening.

But it was the sixth rose that sent an atavistic chill down her spine. She found it on her pillow that night as she turned back the covers of the bed.

Lucian Hawk had been there, standing beside her bed, sometime during the day.

It was a long time before Ariana went to sleep that night, and it seemed as though she had just barely managed the feat of getting her eyes closed when she was awakened at four in the morning with an irrational thought. If Lucian Hawk were to fall in love, would he know how to go about asking for love in return? Or would he try to force a response by utilizing his magician's bag of tricks? She went back to sleep again before she could ponder the significance of the question.

The call from Richard Dearborn came at ten the next morning, and even as she accepted it, Ariana was forced to realize that a part of her had hoped it would be a call from Lucian.

"Ariana," Richard began in his pleasant, well-cultivated voice, "I'm going to have to leave for New York on a business trip in the morning. Any chance you could have dinner with me tonight?"

The first thing that popped into her mind as she listened to the invitation was Lucian's warning about the dangers of angering a magician. The second thing that came into her head was a grim, reckless desire to reestablish her independence from the man who had deceived her this weekend. Damn it! She most certainly did not belong to Lucian Hawk, whatever he might think!

"I'd love to, Richard," she heard herself saying smoothly. "What time?"

"I'll pick you up at seven, darling. We'll go down to the Wharf. Mario is promising to hold some fresh swordfish for us and an excellent Chardonnay. How does that sound?"

"It sounds wonderful, Richard. I'll look forward to it."

And she honestly did try to look forward to their date, but even as she dressed carefully in a violet blue pleated column of a dress that fell narrowly over her slender figure, Ariana kept wondering what Lucian Hawk was doing and what he would say if he knew that she was seeing Richard.

Richard Dearborn was at his most urbane and charming that evening, clearly looking forward with anticipation to a successful business trip the following day. Ariana did her best to make conversation, trying to keep her mind off the realization that with this man she would never find the spark that had ignited so easily between herself and Lucian. Something just wasn't right.

There was no magic with Richard Dearborn, she finally told herself wryly as the evening drew to a close. And after having had a sample of the real thing, she no longer wanted to content herself with a pleasant facade. Ariana wanted the magic.

What had Lucian done to her? How could she have allowed such a man to disrupt her life to such an extent? Why couldn't she put him out of her mind and out of her life?

"I hate to have to take you home so early, Ari," Richard sighed as he assisted her into a cab, "but I've got to leave at six tomorrow morning. Don't hold it against me, darling. I promise I'll make it up to you when I return."

"Don't worry about it, Richard. As a matter of fact I've had rather a difficult day and need some sleep. Have a good trip to New York," she responded as the cab drew up in front of her door.

"I'll see you inside," Richard said gallantly, signaling to the driver to wait. He climbed out of the cab and escorted Ariana to her door. As she turned the key in the lock and pushed it slightly ajar, he took her into his arms.

Ariana felt his lips on hers in a sophisticated, polished embrace, and all she could think about was the magic she had known when Lucian had held her.

"Good night, Richard," she whispered almost sadly as he took his leave. She felt as if she were really saying good-bye. Whatever happened, she would not tie herself in marriage to Richard Dearborn. She knew that now with stoic resignation. In fact, she had known it earlier that evening when she had dressed for him. Lucian's impact on her senses had left no room for another man.

That realization was occupying her thoughts as she reached out to flip on the foyer light switch.

"Have a nice evening, Ariana?"

For an instant she thought her mind had conjured him up out of thin air. Ariana froze in the doorway, her hand still on the switch as dappled light from the faceted globe overhead illuminated Lucian's dark figure lounging in the arched entrance to the living room.

"Lucian!"

He regarded her with a raking gaze. Even though he was leaning almost casually against the wall, his arms folded across his chest, one foot crossed over the other, all Ariana could think about was the peril of offending a magician.

Lucian Hawk was coldly, dangerously furious.

"At least you had the good sense not to bring him inside," he drawled.

From out of nowhere it seemed, Ariana managed to recover her nearly stifled voice. Behind the lenses of her designer glasses her smoky eyes were wide and wary. The door was still open behind her and some sixth sense urged her to leave it that way.

"What are you doing here, Lucian?"

"Waiting for you, naturally." He straightened and took a step forward. Instantly Ariana moved backward a pace until she was standing on the threshold outside her own door. Lucian halted, topaz eyes glittering angrily. "Come inside and close the door, Ariana."

"Not unless you'll give me your word you're not going to harm me!"

He appeared to consider that. "I ought to beat you."

"Lucian!" She stared at him, appalled. There was enough tension in the way he stood before her to make her believe him capable of it.

"But I won't," he went on heavily. "I will remind myself that beating you would only serve to reenforce your already low opinion of my background and morals."

Something about the way he said that made Ariana long to tell him that she really didn't have a low opinion of him. Before she could stop to think, she had stepped back into the foyer and was closing the door behind her. "Lucian, I don't know what you hope to accomplish by materializing inside my apartment in this way," she tried to say with a coolness she was far from feeling, "but I can guarantee you that I'm not going to applaud the act!" She tossed her evening bag down on a nearby table and faced him.

"What did you hope to accomplish by going out with Dearborn?" he grated. Dressed in charcoal slacks and a black chamois shirt, he was a dark, intimidating figure standing amid the French vanilla and papaya shades of her apartment.

"I went out with Richard because I wanted to go out with him! I've been dating him frequently for over a month!" Ariana stormed.

"You went out with him because you knew it would infuriate me! He was the strongest weapon you could find to use against me, wasn't he?"

"I don't need a weapon against you!"

"No, you don't *need* one, but you wanted one, didn't you?" Lucian came a step closer. "Did it work, Ariana? Can Dearborn make you forget Saturday night?"

Ariana flinched. Nothing on earth would ever make her forget that night, and she knew from the gleaming gold of Lucian's eyes that he was aware of it. Because he would never forget it, either? Somehow, Ariana desperately wanted that to be the case.

"This is a pointless discussion, Lucian," she managed to say very steadily. "What are you doing here?"

He arched one black brow. "My original reason for stopping by was to give you some information on Fletcher Galen. We're still partners in that little enterprise, remember?''

''I remember,'' she whispered shakily.

''But that can wait,'' he went on grimly. ''When I got here and realized you were gone for the evening I had a hunch you were out somewhere trying to show me that you can do as you please with other men. So I decided I'd hang around until you got back. I think we need to get a couple of things clear between us.''

''Such as?'' she dared, her head lifting haughtily.

''Such as the fact that whatever else happens between you and me, neither of us is going to use someone else as a shield.'' He took another step forward and quite suddenly he had his strong fingers curved around her shoulders. Ariana was trapped. ''Damn it, you know you don't want him,'' he rasped harshly. ''If he'd been important, you would have been sleeping with him long before I came on the scene.''

''That's a typical male conclusion!'' she flung back. ''I'm building a relationship with Richard. One that might end in marriage. I have no wish to rush such an important event. Just because you find it necessary to take a woman to bed after knowing her only a couple of days, that doesn't mean all men work the same way!''

''Only those of us who crawled up out of the gutter the hard way? You could be right,'' he went on as she tried to freeze him with a glance. ''I expect I do work a little differently from Dearborn. But that's because I've learned that moving quickly is the only sure way to get what you want in life. And I want you, Ariana Warfield. I want you so badly I'm not going to take a chance on losing you by playing the game your way."

"I'm not playing a game, Lucian! Damn you! Let me go. Say what you have to say about Fletcher Galen and then leave. It's late and I want to go to bed."

Too late she realized that goading him verbally was probably not the best way of handling an irate magician. She saw the flicker in his golden eyes a scant second before he moved, and then there was no time to escape. His hands slipped down her body and under her thighs. In an instant she was swept off her feet and high in his arms.

"Going to bed is exactly what I had on the agenda for this evening," Lucian assured her in an intense and velvet dark voice that ruffled all her nerve endings. "It seems to be the most efficient method of communicating with you!"

"Put me down." Ariana's arm rested on the black chamois cloth that covered his shoulder as she glared defiantly up into his set features. "I mean it, Lucian. Let me go this instant. I won't allow you to manhandle me this way!"

He turned with her in his arms and started across the living room to the hall that led to her bedroom. "I'm not going to hurt you, Ariana, and you know it. I'm going to make you feel what you felt on Saturday night. And afterward, when you're all soft and glowing in my arms, we'll talk."

"Why, you arrogant bastard," she breathed as her pulse began to race. "If you think I'm going to melt in your arms after the way you've behaved this evening, you're out of your mind."

"Probably. You've had me half out of my mind for almost a week." He strode down the hall and turned into her bedroom with an assurance that made Ariana recall he'd been there once before when he'd left the rose. And that thought brought with it another. But it was too late and in any event there was little she could have done to hide the evidence.

Reaching out to turn on the wall switch with the hand that extended from under Ariana's back, Lucian saw the half-dozen roses in the crystal vase beside her bed as soon as the lamp flared into brightness. Ariana had a moment in which to regret the impulsive way in which she had preserved the six roses he had materialized for her and then she felt the tightening of his arms.

Desperately trying to think of some scathing dismissal of the obvious fact that the roses had meant something far too important to her, Ariana said tightly, "It seemed a shame to just throw them out."

"Ariana," he got out hoarsely, ignoring her faint defense. "I really should beat you for putting me through so much hell!" Then his mouth came down on hers in a fiercely possessive kiss.

Ariana tried to think as he took control of her mouth. She tried to think about her ambivalent feelings toward this man. She tried to think of what a perfect escort Richard Dearborn had been that evening. She tried to think of how angry she should have been with Lucian Hawk. But all she succeeded in thinking about was the undeniable fact that she was back once again in the presence of magic. Real magic.

Her fingers, which rested at the nape of his neck, found themselves entwined in the black and silver of his hair, the gold and crimson nails providing a sensuous contrast. Her lips parted beneath the onslaught of his mouth, allowing him into the warmth he sought.

She was barely aware of being carried the rest of the way to the bed. There was the sensation of softness under her as her back touched the plush papaya-colored spread, and then there was only the hardness of Lucian's body as he followed her down onto the bed.

"My God, woman, you don't have a prayer of escaping me tonight, not after I've seen those roses!" He grated the words against the curve of her throat. "Tell me why you saved them. *Tell me!*"

But she couldn't tell him. She didn't want to take the step of admitting aloud that she was so far under Lucian's spell. Instead she moaned something unintelligible into his shoulder and encircled his neck with her arms.

He seemed willing to take the response as sufficient answer. His teeth nipped with teasing passion, and then his tongue came out to soothe as he found the fastening of her violet blue gown. The solid feel of him beat at her senses, making her totally aware of his mounting desire. One heavy thigh lay across her own, anchoring her on the bedspread so that he could touch her at his pleasure.

Ariana was held in sensual captivity as the pleated dress was lowered to her waist. She heard his muffled groan as he followed the retreating line of the soft fabric with his lips. Her unconfined breasts seemed to swell to fill his hand as he touched her.

"Ariana, my Magic Lady, I could never give you up. Didn't you realize that? I've waited too long to find you!"

"Oh, Lucian," she breathed brokenly. Already the swirling tension of passion was staring to tangle her in its coils. She knew a tightening in her lower body that brought warmth and dampness in its wake. Ariana's nails began to test the resilient muscles of her lover's back, following the contours down to where the chamois shirt disappeared into his slacks.

When Lucian pulled away a few inches to finish removing the pleated dress, Ariana closed her eyes and slid her fingers into the waistband of his black slacks. She felt him remove her glasses and toss them along with his own onto the nightstand, and then he was back beside her, whispering heated encouragement.

"Undress me, Magic Lady. Let me feel your fingers in all the right places. I haven't been able to get the memory of your touch out of my head!"

As if to punish her gently for having haunted his mind, Lucian caught one nipple between his teeth and tugged carefully. The resulting sensation sent tremor after tremor through Ariana's body.

''Your body knows what it wants,'' he growled in satisfaction as the nipple grew hard and tight under his caress. ''Listen to your body, Ariana.''

She moaned his name again and fumbled with the buckle of his belt. As if he were suddenly too impatient to wait for her awkward movements, Lucian lifted himself away and pulled off the clothing he wore. She lay looking up at him through her lashes as he stood for a moment beside the bed. Inwardly Ariana acknowledged that the insistent need of her body to know the totality of him was a heady drug. No other man had ever succeeded in drugging her senses like this. Drugging them or casting a spell over them?

He lay alongside her, pressing himself into her hip so that she knew the fullness of his arousal. Gathering her against him with one arm, Lucian flattened his palm at the base of her throat and slowly drew his hand downward. It grazed each breast in turn and then glided over her stomach to the upper edge of the small silken garment that was all she still wore.

Lucian raised his head from her throat to look down into her face as he deliberately moved his palm across the triangle of satiny nylon to the warmth between her legs.

''Oh!'' Her gasp was involuntary as he began to draw delicate circles on the surface of the thin material. The exquisite sensation was conducted through the fabric the way electricity was conducted through water. And it had almost the same effect. Ariana writhed beneath the touch.

"I can feel the heat in you, Magic lady," he rasped. "Already you're hot and warm and sweetly damp. I couldn't leave you now if I tried."

He rolled on top of her, thrusting provocatively against the nylon that still barred the path. Ariana cried out softly as she felt her body respond to the knowledge that he waited at the gate. Instinctively she arched her hips, only to know a pulsating frustration as the nylon of her underwear continued to prohibit his entrance.

For some reason the teasing sensation made her go wild in his arms. It was as if, having realized that she couldn't have him within her immediately, she suddenly *had* to have him. Her senses clamored for the release only he could provide.

"Lucian, oh, Lucian, *please,*" she begged, arching passionately once more against him.

He caught her wrists gently when she would have lowered her hands to remove the garment that still remained between them. Pinning her hands to the bed on either side of her head, Lucian kissed her deeply, moving his tongue in and out of her mouth in a rhythm which he repeated with his hips.

Ariana shivered and lifted herself against him in a helpless turmoil of desire.

"A little longer, Magic Lady," Lucian muttered thickly in a voice that betrayed his own frayed control. "I want you to know what it feels like to need someone the way I need you.'' He released her wrists and began to explore further.

The sweet torment continued until Ariana was a restless, raging wild thing in his arms. Her senses spun and her passions rioted as he steadfastly provoked her. Her legs wrapped around him, urging him as close as possible and her hands danced a primitive pattern across his back. Ariana thought that she would go mad, and her only consolation was the knowledge that Lucian was very close to losing his iron control. She would push him over the edge and make him finish what he had started if it took all the strength in her body!

"My God, woman! I knew I wouldn't be able to resist you very long in bed, but I thought I could hold out longer than this!"

Sliding one hand down her spine to her hips, Lucian lifted her and slipped off the panties that had barred the way to her softness. Instantly Ariana sucked in her breath and clung, pulling him close. Lucian needed no further urging.

With a deep, husky groan he surged against her body, sheathing himself in her hot, damp warmth. "Yes, Magic Lady, oh, *yes!*"

Then he was riding the storm he had unleashed, inciting it to new heights even as he quickly became its victim. Ariana shut her eyes tightly and abandoned herself to the power that was driving her body. The shimmering magic blossomed around her until she could no longer think at all.

Her body reacted to every touch, every new sensation being visited upon it. Her palms flattened against the curves of his back and her mouth flowered to receive him.

Gradually the intensity built to the bursting point. Ariana sensed the precipice and knew once more that curious instant of panic. As if he felt it approaching and refused to let her succumb to the strange fear of the unknown, Lucian sank his teeth lightly into her lower lip and simultaneously slid his fingers to the rounded cushion of her buttocks. There he clenched with calculated pressure.

Ariana went hurtling over the edge, losing herself entirely in the glittering magic. She heard Lucian's hoarse cry of satisfaction, and then there were only the shifting colors of the dissipating spell as it slowly broke apart and released the two it had held captive.

It was a long time before Ariana felt Lucian's body shift slowly and roll to one side. She opened her eyes to find him watching her with a gaze that revealed undeniable masculine gratification.

"Promise me," he ordered softly with the arrogance of a man who is certain that he is in control of his woman, "that there won't be any more nights in which I'll have to pace the floor waiting for you to come home from a date with Dearborn or anyone else!" Lucian drew a fingertip up along her throat to the corner of her vulnerable mouth as she lay watching him.

Ariana didn't have the energy to attempt a lie, so she told him the stark truth. "I won't be going out with Richard again." She had known that much when she'd stood on her doorstep and watched the other man drive off in the cab. There didn't seem much point in trying to pretend otherwise to Lucian.

He let out a long sigh of satisfaction that might have been tinged with relief. "So that much is settled, at least." He leaned over and brushed a surprisingly tender kiss against her lips. "Ariana, there's something I want to explain to you," he went on slowly as he lifted his head again.

"Yes, Lucian?"

Lucian's mouth was edged with the smile of a man who is about to indulge his lover and is already anticipating her delight. His eyes were soft and full of his own pleasure. "You told me once that marriage was on your list of demands. You said you wouldn't consider an affair. I told you I wasn't interested either in marriage or in signing your damn prenuptial agreement. You've explained why you were trying to insist on a safe marriage. Well, now I'd like to explain why I told you I wasn't about to marry again. And why I'm having some second thoughts."

"Second thoughts?" she queried uncertainly.

"Oh, not about that business with the contract. I'm not about to sign anything like that," he assured her gruffly, "but with you I think I would take another chance on marriage." His smile widened as he waited for her reaction.

But Ariana merely smiled in return and closed his mouth with the tips of her fingers as she sat up beside him. "That's all right, Lucian. You don't have to explain anything to me."

"I want to, Ariana," he insisted, the first hint of a frown pulling his dark brows together as she turned away to sit up on the edge of the bed.

"It's not necessary, Lucian," she said, glancing back over her bare shoulder with the expression of a woman who is surrendering totally to the idea of an affair and is demanding nothing in return. "I've dropped my demand for marriage along with all my other demands. You don't have to worry about it anymore. I'm not going to go on fighting you. I can't. I won't ask for marriage."

She got to her feet and reached for the robe that hung inside her closet door. As she belted it around her narrow waist she hurried to the bathroom and shut herself inside. With fingers that fumbled violently she switched on the taps in the shower and stuffed her hair up under her cap. Her whole body was trembling with the tension of anticipation.

The bang of the bathroom door being thrown open behind her came just as she was about to step behind the striped shower curtain. Ariana turned to face a chillingly furious Lucian. For an instant they stared at each other across the short distance separating them, and Ariana felt her heart pound as she acknowledged the enormity of what she was doing and the violence of his reaction to her words.

"Are you telling me," Lucian grated in a deadly soft voice, "that I'm not good enough to marry?"

Eight

"I didn't say you weren't good enough to marry, Lucian, and I certainly wasn't implying any such thing!" Feeling terribly vulnerable as she stood nude on the threshold of the shower, Ariana took the only escape possible and stepped behind the plastic curtain. The bold, lean maleness of him seemed to dominate the pastel bathroom.

Good lord! She ought to have foreseen that potential reaction! What was the matter with her? Couldn't she have guessed he'd take her lack of interest in marriage as an insult? It was just that in the soft aftermath of his lovemaking she had finally convinced herself that he cared for her. There was an elemental quality about Lucian Hawk that told her he wasn't playing tricks, not on the fundamental level of their strange relationship.

When he had gone so far as to mention marriage she had decided to take the biggest risk of her life and gently fling the offer back in his face.

She wanted marriage, Ariana admitted freely to herself, but she didn't want it presented to her indulgently as a reward for her surrender the way news of Lucian's financial status had been presented. Ariana had no intention of marrying Lucian Hawk unless he wanted the binding tie as much as she did.

Lucian had to learn how to ask for love.

The conviction was firm in her mind, but Ariana was honest enough, even in those first moments of arriving at the decision, to acknowledge that she was gambling for very high stakes. What if she were wrong about her magician? What if he didn't feel anything more than mere desire? What if passion was all he required from her?

The only way she would ever learn the truth of his feelings for her was to let him discover for himself that an affair was not enough. The realization of what she was doing sent a small shiver through Ariana. There had been warnings aplenty about the dangers of angering a magician. What kind of penalties existed for a woman who tried to use the contents of her own bag of tricks against him?

The shower curtain was rudely swept aside as Lucian stepped inside the tiled stall. A quick sidelong glance revealed that he was far from convinced of the sincerity of her words a moment earlier. He reached to catch hold of Ariana's arms, his face set in uncompromising lines. She was vividly conscious of his raw masculinity.

"If you think for one minute that you can have an affair with me while you wait for a proposal from a more suitable candidate," he ground out roughly, "you're in for one hell of a shock!"

"There's no need to play the heavy-handed male," Ariana managed in a soothing tone. Daring to lift her hand to his cheek, she stroked it with a featherlight touch. Her eyes were soft and luminous. "I have no intention of trying to find another man. I told you I believe in fidelity. I'm simply attempting to tell you that you've won. You and my aunt and my brother are all right and I was wrong. There is no reason to insist on a marriage license. We're two adult people who should be able to give our word to each other and keep it. I was only seeking marriage and a wedding contract as a way of protecting myself. I suppose it was a way of asking a man to prove himself. But there's no need to do that with you, is there? You're certainly no threat financially, and I think I can trust you in other ways. You'll be honest and straightforward with me when the time comes that you decide you no longer want me?"

He frowned ferociously. "Sweetheart, you're the only woman I want. For God's sake, of course you can trust me!"

"Then there's no reason for this argument, is there?" she whispered and stood on tiptoe to kiss the taut line of his mouth.

Instantly he wrapped his arms around her and

swept her close against his wet, muscled frame, his mouth putting her butterfly kiss through a passionate metamorphosis. It emerged as a breathless, clinging embrace that left Ariana feeling thoroughly branded.

"God knows the last thing I want to do with you tonight is argue!" The statement came with great depth of feeling as Lucian reluctantly broke the sensual contact. His palms slipped down her shoulders to cover her breasts as his eyes met hers. "But I want to explain why I've been so cautious about marriage."

"You said you were married once?"

He nodded. "A long time ago. She was very beautiful, and I was just beginning to make something of myself. She seemed perfect to me, like a lovely doll. Just the right woman to have beside me as I made my fortune. When she insisted on marriage I didn't argue. Unfortunately I discovered too late that a perfect little doll was just exactly what she was. Beautiful but incapable of caring about anyone other than herself. When she met me I was the most successful man she knew. A year of marriage to me, however, put her into contact with several men who were far more successful than I was at the time. I came home from work one day to find she'd filed for divorce in order to marry one of them. Frankly I was glad to see her go. The whole experience left a sour taste in my mouth for the noble institution of marriage, however."

"And so you became very wary of women who seemed somewhat mercenary, hmmm?" Ariana smiled serenely, her fingers splayed against his chest. "I understand, Lucian." Deliberately she brushed the topic aside. "There's something you should know about tonight, though. I didn't date Richard with the intention of punishing you."

"No?" He looked skeptical.

She shook her head firmly. "I think I just wanted to make one last comparison before I accepted the inevitable."

"And what was the result of your 'comparison'?" he demanded with a returning touch of aggression.

"Just that there is no magic for me with Richard. There's never been any real magic for me with anyone except you," she told him simply.

"Ariana!" He pulled her close again, burying his face against the wet skin of her neck. She felt him shudder. "You won't regret this, sweetheart. I'll make it all right, I swear!"

The subject of marriage was dropped, and Ariana didn't know whether to be pleased or depressed.

With the contented humor of a large, satiated jungle cat Lucian turned what remained of the shower into a teasing frolic that finally drove Ariana to seek a laughing escape. She stepped out of the shower, grabbing for one of the thick towels on the rack, and left him to finish by himself.

"When you come out I want to hear what you discovered about Fletcher Galen," she called as she slipped back into her robe and went to the door.

"Oh, yeah. I almost forgot. I guess I got side-tracked," he called back.

"Uh huh." Ariana's mouth crooked wryly as she opened the bathroom door and stepped out into the hall.

By the time he had emerged from her bedroom wearing only his charcoal slacks, Ariana was waiting in the kitchen. She'd made a pot of hot chocolate and had put out a plate of cookies.

Lucian accepted the offering with alacrity, reaching for three of the little cookies as he sat down. "I put a good private investigative service on Galen two days ago."

"Is that his real name? Fletcher Galen?" Ariana asked curiously as she sat down across from him.

"Yeah, surprisingly enough. He's got a couple of other names apparently, but Galen is the one he uses when he's running the 'Contact-an-Extraterrestrial' scam." Lucian reached for his cup of hot chocolate.

"He's gotten away with this before?" Ariana was disgusted.

"Apparently he tried something similar down in Arizona a year ago. Bilked a lot of retirees of several thousand dollars over the course of a few weeks."

"Why doesn't someone stop him?"

"A lot of people won't file a complaint or testify. They're too embarrassed at having been taken in so easily. Also, Galen keeps on the move. By the time the Arizona authorities became aware of him, he'd skipped. This kind of con game is amazingly common, honey. The first-class con artists often operate with impunity for years. Even when they are caught they rarely go to jail. They just jump bail and head for South America or somewhere until things cool down.''

"How does Galen's scam work? Is he making his money off those horrendously high fees he charges?'' Ariana asked, frowning.

"No, the fees are just established to keep out the riff-raff,'' Lucian told her dryly. ''When the pitch is made for money, Galen wants to be sure he's hitting the right crowd, people who can afford it.''

"Those large checks my aunt has been drawing on her account?'' Ariana pressed.

"If this scam is like the one he pulled in Arizona, your aunt and the others have been donating toward a 'research' facility which will be used to set up continuing contact with Krayton after the initial breakthrough has been made.''

"Oh, my God! And Aunt Philomena fell for this?''

"According to the investigator I hired, a lot of people have. And when Galen skips town with their money most won't complain.''

"They'll be too humiliated over having been duped.'' Ariana sighed. ''I know the feeling. How are we going to explain all this to Aunt Phil?''

"The investigator is compiling a lot of documentary evidence like the articles which ran in the Arizona papers after the last operation and reports the authorities made, that sort of thing. He's going to collect what he can and then we'll show it to Phil. That's about all we can do, unless…''

Ariana narrowed her eyes as he let the sentence trail off thoughtfully. ''Unless what?''

Lucian shrugged. "Well, it might be interesting to see what the audience's reaction would be if Galen's performance failed to come off as scheduled one night during a session," he said slowly.

"What are you suggesting?" Ariana waited breathlessly, her eyes lighting up with anticipation.

"You have to understand that people are very odd in their reactions to the kind of evidence the investigator is going to come up with," he began carefully. "A lot of them will tend to dismiss it as yellow journalism or deliberate slander. If they want to go on believing, they will. But the one thing a magician can't survive is the embarrassment of tricks that go awry."

"If things go wrong during a performance, couldn't he just claim that proper contact hadn't been made?"

"Not if things go wrong in an embarrassing fashion," Lucian drawled, his eyes concentrating on some point in the middle distance as he ran several things through his mind.

"You said that if you were to leap up during the middle of a performance, you'd probably be subdued by those characters in the monk suits," she reminded him worriedly.

"I'm not suggesting I pull anything quite that grand. The essence of a good piece of magic is adequate preparation. I'm suggesting that I help Galen prepare for one of his performances."

Ariana went very still as she sensed the direction

of his thoughts. "You're going to tamper with his bag of tricks?"

"Ummm. It could produce some interesting results."

"But to do that you'd have to get inside that compound, and once inside the gates you'd have to get into the room where he conducts those séances."

"Exactly." He brought his attention back to her face and smiled wryly at her expression of dismay. "It shouldn't be any more complicated than getting that rose onto your office chair."

"Lucian! Are you serious?" she whispered, her mouth suddenly very dry as she remembered the forbidding gates and the hooded men who walked inside the compound.

"I think it's worth a look. What do you say we drive back to the inn tomorrow afternoon, arranging to arrive around nightfall?"

"I don't want you taking any chances!" she declared.

He grinned, a wicked magician's grin, and the topaz eyes gleamed. "The only dangerous chances I've taken lately are with a reckless little red-haired witch who has nearly driven me out of my mind. Compared with those hazards, getting into Galen's setup and rearranging his performance should be child's play!"

Ariana gasped as he lunged to his feet, reached around the table, caught her wrist and dragged her into a tumble on his lap. With one arm cradling her, Lucian continued to munch cookies. "Tell me what made you save the roses, Ariana," he challenged.

She lifted a hand with deliberate vagueness. "I told you. They were too pretty to throw away."

"I don't believe you," he announced complacently. "Tell me the truth."

That she was wildly, heedlessly in love with him? Not a chance, Ariana decided resolutely. She had done all the surrendering she intended to do. Sooner or later Lucian Hawk was going to have to learn that love was a two-way street and that each party took some risks.

"There's nothing to tell, Lucian, except that I suppose I knew as I collected each rose that you were becoming more and more inevitable." That much was true, she reflected. Ariana ran her fingers through his tousled dark hair and smiled up at him. "How does a woman defend herself against a magician?" she asked whimsically.

"I couldn't leave you any defense," he said quietly, his eyes turning very serious. "I wanted you too much to take a chance on your escaping me."

"Did you, Lucian?"

He swallowed the last of the cookie, and then he nudged her chin with the edge of his hand and lifted her mouth for his kiss. "Damn right," he muttered. Then he was surging to his feet with her in his arms.

"Lucian?"

"I'm going to take you back to bed and show you some nifty sleight-of-hand," he explained as he strode down the hall.

Ariana nestled her head against his bare shoulder and gave herself up to what remained of the night.

In the morning she would deal once more with the future. The night belonged to the magician.

Lucian picked Ariana up late the next afternoon in a dark green Jaguar. He was dressed in faded jeans and a chocolate brown corduroy shirt. Suitable clothing for sneaking around the camps of enemy magicians, Ariana thought nervously. The closer the trip had approached, the more anxious she had become. Even a quick visit to talk things over with her brother had not allayed her fears. As she went down the front steps to meet Lucian, her brows were drawn together in a severe line.

"Nothing like having your woman greet you with a radiant smile the day after," he drawled, his eyes roving appreciatively over her designer jeans and royal blue sweater. He leaned down to kiss her firmly. "Cheer up, honey, nothing's going to go wrong!"

"Famous last words! Listen, Lucian. I've been thinking about this…"

"Heaven help us," he teased.

"I'm serious! If you're determined to go through with this, then I'm going to wait in the car while you sneak inside the compound. We'll synchronize our watches, and if you don't return at the agreed-upon time, I'm going to go for help!"

"There's no need to synchronize our watches," he pointed out amiably as he started the engine of the Jaguar. "We're both wearing quartz watches. They keep time almost perfectly."

"Don't tease me, Lucian!"

"Okay. If you want to wait in the car and stand prepared to go for the cavalry, you can. I don't see any problem with that. Just promise me you won't jump the gun!"

"Tell me how much time you think you'll need, and I'll wait exactly that long."

"An hour and a half should do it. Probably won't take that much time." He shifted smoothly for a stoplight and turned to flick her a laughing-eyed glance. "You're really worried, aren't you?"

Ariana, who had been worried all day, glowered at him. "And you're really enjoying this, aren't you?" she tossed back.

"Makes a pleasant change of pace from real estate."

"Lucian?"

"Hmmm?

"How did you get inside my office that night to leave the rose?"

"I'll tell you on our first anniversary," he promised.

"Since we're not going to be getting married, I think that's too long to have to wait," she retorted firmly, repressing a spark of hope.

"Ariana, you were the one who wanted to get married," he reminded her in a neutral tone.

"I've changed my mind," she declared with false breeziness. "Who needs it?" Then she hurried to shift the topic again. "Are we going to stop for a snack somewhere on the way or are you going to perform your walking through walls trick on an empty stomach?''

He frowned as if not particularly pleased at the direction of the conversation and then he asked politely, ''I take it you're hungry?''

''You're a mind reader!''

''Actually, I never went in for that kind of magic,'' he said wryly. ''It takes an assistant and I prefer to work alone.''

''How do they do those mind-reading acts where one person goes down into the audience and the mind reader is blindfolded on stage?'' she demanded.

''Codes,'' he explained easily. ''That's why it takes two people. The person who goes down into the audience has to communicate with the mind reader by a variety of subtle codes. If she holds up a man's gold watch, for instance, she might say something like, 'Tell me quickly, quickly, what I'm holding in my hand.' The mind reader knows that 'quickly, quickly' is a code for gold watch. The codes can get extremely elaborate, depending on how well the two performers can memorize. Sometimes silent codes are used. Electronic gadgets and such. It can get very involved.''

''And what about some of the other famous tricks? How about the one where a woman is sawed in half inside a box?'' Ariana asked eagerly, sensing he was in a communicative mood.

''There are a variety of methods. Some revolve around having a table that is quite deep beneath the box. It doesn't look deep enough to hold a second woman, but that's because the edge of the table is beveled out to only a couple of inches. The center is actually thick enough to hold the second person, and there's a trap door in the bottom of the box.''

"So the second woman can put her feet out the opposite end of the box?''

"Right. The first woman is curled up inside the first half of the box. There are other methods, but that's one of the oldest.''

"Okay,'' Ariana went on with relish, "how about all those escapes Houdini did?''

"Well, to begin with, he was an expert on locks. He was also an expert at concealing implements with which to pick locks. Also, the more elaborate a box or a bunch of rope ties or chains are, the more opportunities there are for having trick mechanisms for escape built into the apparatus.''

"Why is it his name that everyone remembers when they're asked to name a famous magician? What was so special about his performances?''

"It's hard to say. He was a fabulous showman and he had a flair for dramatic, death-defying stunts. There have been whole books written on why his name lives on, but no one can really put it into words. He was a magician,'' Lucian concluded simply.

"He made a practice of exposing spiritualists and psychics, didn't he?''

"Yes, for all the good it did. The people who wanted to believe kept right on believing, Ariana. That's a blunt fact of human nature. We may succeed in persuading your aunt that Galen's a fraud, but you can bet that even if I manage to have him make a fool of himself in front of the audience, several members of it will still go on believing in him. Right up to the point where their money disappears and Galen skips town!''

They stopped for a quick supper, and half an hour before they reached their destination, night began to fall heavily around the mountains. Lucian briefly explained his plans. Ariana was aware of the increasing tension in him. It wasn't a nervous tension, rather the anticipatory heightening of awareness that a man might experience prior to going before an audience or into battle. She stirred restlessly on her side of the car as second and third thoughts assailed her.

"Lucian, maybe we should call this off."

"Would you rather I took you to the inn, first?" he offered dryly.

"No!"

"Okay, then stop suggesting we call it off. It's too late for that."

"Are you going to tell Aunt Phil you've rigged Galen's performance?"

"It's going to be pretty damn obvious someone's interfered with it." Lucian grinned. It was a feral sort of grin and Ariana didn't care for it. "I think we'll stop by the compound first. I'll make my little adjustments to Galen's bag of tricks, and then we'll drive on to the inn. Everyone there should be just about finished with dinner and preparing to go the séance. We'll attend along with the others. Yes, I think I will warn Phil, but no one else. If Galen got wind of my tampering in time, he might be able to salvage the act. Phil will keep quiet and let the chips fall where they may.''

Ariana nodded. ''Yes, she'll be willing to give him a fair test.''

It was quite dark when Lucian pulled the Jaguar well off the road several hundred yards from the secluded retreat. He parked out of sight and turned in the seat to deliver last minute instructions to Ariana.

''Remember, no panicking. Everything's going to be fine, but it could be one hell of an embarrassment for me if you get nervous and go for help!'' he lectured sternly.

''Then you'd better not be late getting back to the car,'' she retorted grimly. ''I'd rather see you embarrassed than hurt!''

''It's nice to know you care,'' he drawled gently. ''Ariana, when this is all over I really don't see any reason why we shouldn't go ahead and get married. What difference would it make? And I know you'd be more comfortable with a ring on your finger.''

''Nonsense,'' she scoffed with credible nonchalance. ''I'm not even going to get any family pressure to legalize things, remember? My aunt and my brother don't believe in the necessity of marriage, and I know how you feel about it. Relax, Lucian. I've come around to your way of thinking. Now off you go and take care of yourself,'' she urged.

He scowled at her for a long moment, and then with a violent little wrench he opened the Jaguar's door and stepped outside into the night. Leaning down, he said, ''Sit in the driver's seat with the key in the ignition in case something comes up and we have to leave quickly. And keep the doors locked until you see me, understand?''

''I understand.'' She slid across into the driver's seat as Lucian straightened and slammed the car door. A moment later he was lost in the shadows of the surrounding forest.

Almost at once the darkness and quiet seemed to close around the Jaguar. Ariana glanced at her watch and knew that she would do so again and again as she waited for Lucian to reappear. She recalled Drake's words of advice to her that morning and smiled wanly. All she could do was sit and wait.

For lack of anything more productive she thought about the idea of marrying Lucian Hawk. Damn it, she wasn't going to let him do her any favors! If Lucian wanted marriage, it would have to be because he loved her so much he wanted all the trimmings. Not because he wanted to indulge and reward her for giving herself to him.

She knew that she was taking a terrible risk by pushing him this way. If he wasn't genuinely in love with her and was concerned only with possession, then he would grow bored with attempting to do her the favor of marriage. He would be content with an affair.

If that was the way things worked out, Ariana knew that she was going to be devastated. She wanted so much to believe that Lucian was in love with her as deeply as she was in love with him. She wanted him to comprehend his own feelings, and that, she knew, was asking a lot. She had the feeling that Lucian had made a habit of reaching out and taking what he wanted in life. He had probably rarely been called upon to analyze his own emotions very thoroughly. He knew he wanted her, but did he know that what he really wanted was her love, not just her passion and warmth?

For that matter, Ariana reminded herself sadly, did *she* know that he wanted more than just the physical side of their relationship? She was staking so much on an affirmative answer to that question.

Time was what they needed, she told herself as she sat staring into the shadows. Time to get to know each other well, to become accustomed to the feelings that had sprung up so quickly between them. An affair would give them that time, even though it might end in disaster for her if it turned out that Lucian didn't truly love her.

Ariana didn't see that she had much choice. She had already taken her chances. She had surrendered to him just as he had demanded. Now she could only pray that he would be willing to take the risk of admitting that what bound them together was love. Lucian Hawk had to take a few chances of his own.

Time dragged on as she sat impatiently in the front seat of the Jaguar. Philomena didn't know that they were due to arrive at the inn that evening. Lucian had called for reservations late in the afternoon just before they had left San Francisco, and unless the desk clerk thought to mention the fact to Philomena, she wouldn't be expecting her niece and Lucian.

How would she react when she realized that this time only one room had been requested?

Ariana's mouth curved ruefully at the thought. Two rooms last time had definitely been a waste of money. She was contemplating the memory of that fateful night when the magician, himself, materialized out of the darkness in front of the car.

As he loped toward her she unlocked the car door and slid into the passenger's seat. He looked grimly pleased with himself, she decided, aware of a vast relief that he was safe.

"What happened? How did it go? Did anyone see you? Could you get inside?"

He threw her a wide grin as he turned the key in the ignition. "One question at a time, I've had a hard night!"

"Waiting is much harder work, believe me!" she assured him feelingly. He leaned over and kissed her soundly before putting the powerful car in gear.

"Here, I brought you a little reward for your patience." He dropped a yellow rose into her hand.

"What in the world? Lucian! Where did you get this?"

"Magic," he explained succinctly.

She looked up from the rose as he pulled the car out onto the winding road that led to the inn. "Did you accomplish what you set out to do? Could you find Galen's tricks?"

"I'm afraid our extraterrestrial visitor is going to

be in for a shock tonight when he tries to traverse the spaceways," Lucian chuckled.

"You're really quite pleased with yourself, aren't you?"

"It's going to be an amusing evening, Ariana."

She glanced down again at the rose in her palm. Somehow he had smuggled it all the way from San Francisco, carried it with him when he made the foray to Galen's retreat and had had it ready to produce when he returned to the car.

Magic.

Ariana took a deep breath and told herself that she didn't want him to continue to reward her with this kind of magic. She wanted the real thing: Love.

Nine

Once again Ariana found herself sitting between Philomena and Lucian in pitch darkness. The evening séance conducted by Fletcher Galen was about to begin. Even though she knew that the whole thing was fake and that Lucian had rigged the already-rigged performance, the sensation of uneasy dread was as strong or stronger than it had been the first time. She didn't understand it. Why should she be even more nervous now that she knew how most of the tricks worked?

Philomena leaned over to whisper in her ear, "This is going to be so interesting." The older woman was delighted at the prospect of the drama which was about to unfold. "I can't wait to see which magician is the stronger!"

"It's not a question of which of them is stronger,"

Ariana muttered. "It's a question of whether or not Galen discovered that his pranks had been tampered with before the performance. I suppose you could say it's a matter of which of them is more clever than the other. Not stronger."

"Same difference," Lucian murmured laconically. He reached out and took her hand in his own, and she could hear the indulgent smile in his voice as he went on softly, "What's the matter with you? You're trembling again. Don't you have any faith in the magician on your side?"

"I just wish it was all over!"

"It will be fairly soon now," he assured her gently.

Ariana also wished that she wasn't the only one in the room who seemed to sense some kind of impending danger. It was just a magic show, for heaven's sake, and it was about to go amusingly awry. So why did she feel as if there was a genuine threat hovering in the atmosphere? Only Philomena had been told that she was about to see Galen exposed. None of the other attendees at the séance had any reason to suspect a somewhat different show tonight.

For her part, Philomena had been more than willing to see the challenge carried out. With her bubbling enthusiasm for the extraordinary and the bizarre, she was just as intrigued by the prospect of Galen's being dramatically exposed as by the possibility that he was a genuine psychic with contacts in outer space.

On the other side of her, Lucian seemed calm, even faintly amused at the prospect of the show that was about to unfold.

Ariana shivered and wondered again why she was the only one who was so nervous.

Then there was no longer any time to reflect on her premonition of danger. The eerie green glow on the stage slowly bloomed into existence, and the audience hushed with expectation. After a suitably dramatic pause Fletcher Galen appeared with the timing of a real showman. His robes swirled around his feet as if disturbed by an invisible wind. The movement gave an appearance of crackling energy surrounding him.

"Offstage fan," Lucian whispered dryly as Ariana stared. "A new addition to the repertoire, apparently."

"My brothers and sisters who are the Keepers of the Energy," Galen intoned, "tonight there is raw power in the very air around us. Tonight great strides can be made. Tonight, perhaps, will be the breakthrough night. We must concentrate together, focus on the power within and without. We must form a channel for Krayton!"

Ariana stirred restlessly as Galen continued with the dramatic patter. When the tray of items scheduled to be broken or levitated was brought forth she felt Lucian's fingers tighten fractionally around hers.

"Now we'll see how good Krayton is when confronted by a little household glue," he growled in anticipation.

On stage Galen went through the ritual of building the "energy" that he'd told his audience was practically arcing through the room that night.

"We must not rush," the fraudulent psychic cautioned his audience as he prepared to bend and break silverware with the power of Krayton. "Great power must be controlled and channeled. We must guide it through the routes we have been establishing for the past few weeks."

Slowly, with grand emphasis, Galen moved his hand over the tray of objects. The audience held its breath, even though they'd seen variations on this particular trick several times previously.

When nothing happened, the reaction from the onlookers was one of stunned dismay. A gasp of disappointment seemed to emanate as if from one throat.

Philomena Warfield merely watched with fascination and then reached over to prod her niece in the ribs. "Interesting. First time this particular event has ever failed. Your magician may be the stronger."

"It's going to be interesting to see how he talks himself out of the problem," Lucian whispered blandly.

Fletcher Galen was more than equal to the occasion. He immediately launched into an explanation for the failure of the trick. "Too much power!" he exclaimed in tones of ringing wonder. "There is too much power in the room. Krayton does not dare to loose it on such small efforts. It might literally explode if channeled too tightly! We must move on.

The energy has built up even more than I had dreamed!''

A low murmur rippled through the room, but the audience seemed willing to buy the explanation. At once Galen moved on to the next piece of magic in his act.

But the direction of the evening had been firmly established by Lucian's tampering. One after the other the magic tricks failed. Galen managed to hold his audience with explanations of energy and uncontrolled power, but it was obvious that he was getting harried.

"I just hope he doesn't quit before he gets to the good part," Lucian said dryly into Ariana's ear.

The hypnotic trance went well for Galen. Lucian had explained ahead of time that there wasn't much he could do about that one. People susceptible to hypnosis would see what Galen wanted them to see. But when the so-called psychic went into his own trance and prepared for levitation, Lucian's hand tightened once again around Ariana's.

Disaster struck. The concealed wires and bracing that were the apparatus behind the trick failed dramatically, sending Galen into an undignified heap on the stage floor.

Shock was the first reaction of the audience. There was nothing that could have stunned it more than to see its cherished psychic sitting unexpectedly on his rear on the stage floor amid a tangle of robes.

"Krayton!" Galen called, lifting his hands to the

ceiling. "What do you want from us tonight? Why is your power being withheld?"

"I'll have to give him credit for being a real trooper right to the end," Lucian chuckled. "Of course, the thought of losing all the money he hopes to get from this audience is probably something of an inspiration."

"Krayton," Galen called again and motioned to the audience to join him in his plea.

At once a cry went up from the confused people watching the debacle of a performance.

"Krayton!"

"Krayton!"

The chant continued as Galen went through more rituals of gathering power.

"He's really damn good with an audience," Lucian said in admiration as the people around them went into a frenzy of desperate chanting. They didn't want to believe the evidence of their own eyes. They wanted an explanation for the failures, and only the mysterious Krayton could give it to them.

"This is the most amusing thing that's happened in a year," Philomena confided cheerfully to Ariana.

Ariana didn't respond. The sense of impending dread was building in her even as the so-called energy around them was being built up in preparation for the dramatic arrival of Krayton.

"Try not to go through the roof," Lucian advised Ariana.

"Why? What's going to happen?" she pleaded urgently, not wanting any more surprises of any kind.

"You'll see."

Lightning crackled dramatically across the room.

"I left the voltage generator alone," Lucian explained as the current arced vividly over the heads of the spectators.

"Oh," Ariana said a little weakly.

Galen called upon Krayton to appear. The audience pleaded with Krayton to make the effort to project himself across the galaxy. Philomena waited with cheerful expectancy. Ariana wanted to cringe as her anxiety mounted, and Lucian lounged in his chair, just waiting for the inevitable.

Lights came on overhead, deeply mysterious lights designed to imitate the imagined colors of another world, and the inhuman face of Krayton began to revolve slowly into view.

The audience shrieked with excitement. Ariana dug her nails into Lucian's hand and felt him wince.

Then Krayton fell into the audience.

Pandemonium broke out and someone at the rear of the room found the light switch. In an instant all was revealed.

The plastic features of the extraterrestrial lay across several quickly vacated seats. Clearly the face of Krayton was a very human bit of creativity. As the lights came on the exotic creature was illuminated, revealing nothing more than cleverly painted plastic dangling from several broken wires.

The strangled gasp of outrage and pain that came from the audience as everyone turned to stare at poor Krayton went like a wave through the room. On its heels, Philomena Warfield rose majestically from her seat and announced to all and sundry, "Well, we certainly have been a pack of fools, haven't we? Thank heaven there are a few honest magicians in this world to help weed out the charlatans like Galen. If it hadn't been for the man who is soon to be my niece's husband, we'd all have been parted from a great deal more of our money, wouldn't we?"

As one, the heads of the audience turned toward the stage. It was quite empty. In the furor, Fletcher Galen had clearly opted to retire as Krayton's power source.

"Come on," Lucian said firmly, rising to his feet and pulling Ariana up beside him. "Let's go. That's the end of the show."

Philomena and Ariana were ushered up the aisle and through the curtain at the opposite end. In the glaring overhead light the mysterious, heretofore dark room was revealed to be only a small theater. Ariana glanced around worriedly. The performance was over, but her sense of disaster was heavier than ever.

"We'll see you to your car, Philomena, and then meet you back at the inn," Lucian instructed, guiding the two women before him.

"This is so exciting!" Philomena declared happily as they joined with the crowd that was milling around in the compound.

There was no sign of the men in monks' clothing who had been so evident earlier in the evening.

"Galen undoubtedly knows how to cut his losses

and pull a genuine disappearing act when things go wrong," Lucian growled as he glanced around the courtyard. "We'll probably never see him again. God knows where he'll show up next."

"Well, I, for one, intend to file a complaint with the authorities just on general principles!" Philomena exclaimed firmly.

"Go ahead. The problem is that the authorities won't be able to find Galen," Lucian sighed as he reached Philomena's Mercedes and assisted her inside.

Philomena had insisted on taking her own car earlier in case Lucian was proved wrong and wanted to leave before she did. Now she smiled brightly up through the open window as he closed the door for her. "You put on quite a show tonight, Lucian. It's going to be interesting having you in the family."

"I wish you would stop saying things like that, Aunt Phil," Ariana hissed, her already taut nerves being tightened further at the references to marriage that Philomena had been making since Lucian's and Ariana's arrival at the inn that evening. The older woman had taken one look at the couple and beamed, apparently drawing her own conclusions. When she learned that they had ordered only one room this time she had been quite certain of the future.

"But, darling," Philomena began soothingly.

"Lucian and I are not getting married, Aunt Phil," Ariana tossed back deliberately. "We're having an affair. Just the kind of affair you've been suggesting I have. How many times am I going to have to explain it to you? Now drive carefully back to the inn. We'll see you in a little while."

Philomena glanced sharply at Lucian's narrowed eyes and shrugged philosophically. "See you soon. And thanks for a most entertaining evening, Lucian."

He nodded once and stepped back as Philomena put the car in gear and joined the line of vehicles exiting rather hastily from the parking area.

"Well, that's about enough excitement for me for one evening," he drawled as he took Ariana's arm and led her across the almost empty lot to where the Jaguar was parked.

"You certainly achieved some dramatic results!" she admitted feelingly. "Did you have any trouble earlier this evening figuring out how to sabotage all that stuff?"

"No, I was pretty sure of how most of the apparatus worked. There was nothing particularly innovative or mysterious about any of it. The only problem was to locate the pulleys and wires and arrange to weaken them."

"How did you get inside the compound and then into that room, though?" she demanded as they neared the car.

"I picked the locks," he said casually, as if it were merely a commonplace skill. "Like Houdini, I've always had an interest in locks. The ones on the gates at the rear of the compound aren't nearly as imposing as those on the front gates. Once inside it was all fairly simple."

"So why don't I have a great feeling of relief that it's all over?" Ariana asked half aloud as Lucian reached to open the car door. Neither of them noticed the movement of several dark shadows beyond the car.

"Perhaps," drawled Fletcher Galen as he emerged from the other side of a hedge, "because it isn't over. Not quite." He was holding a gun in one hand.

Ariana froze, the sense of impending dread finally fulfilled as disaster at last materialized. Beside her Lucian went equally still.

"You'd better get moving, Galen. Some of your fellow Keepers of the Energy are feeling a bit annoyed with you this evening," Lucian said coolly.

"They're all intent on vacating the premises. You and the little lady here are about the only ones left. Except for a few of my staff," he added meaningfully as two of the men in monks' robes appeared on either side of him.

"What do you hope to accomplish?" Lucian asked quietly.

"Nothing much, just a little satisfaction," Galen murmured. "Come here, Miss Warfield."

Ariana didn't move. Galen lifted the gun a little higher and aimed it, not at her, but at Lucian. "Come here or your boyfriend is a dead man. Which would be a pity from your standpoint, because, unless you force me, I really have no intention of killing him. I only want to punish him for interfering in a perfectly good operation."

Ariana sucked in her breath and took a step forward even as Lucian snapped her name tightly between his teeth. She threw him a helpless glance, and then her attention was solely on the gun in Galen's hand.

Her fingers plunged into the pockets of her stylish suede jacket and her head lowered as she took another couple of paces toward Galen. What else could she do? The threat to Lucian was sufficient to bring her into absolute obedience, and she had a hunch that an accomplished con artist like Fletcher Galen knew enough about human nature to recognize the weapon he held over her.

"Very wise, Miss Warfield," Galen growled as she came within reach. In a flash his free arm came out to wrap around her throat and draw her back against his chest.

"Ariana!" Lucian rasped, his face savage in the shadows. The topaz eyes burned as he looked at Galen. "Let her go, Galen. It's me you want."

"Exactly. But I think I have a better chance of keeping you under control as long as I have her. I should have been suspicious that first time you and the little lady attended one of my sessions. But I thought Philomena Warfield was sufficiently hooked and that I could trust her to bring only others who were equally interested in helping poor Krayton cross the universe. In any event, I didn't see much harm in allowing you to stay that first time, even though my staff knew nothing about you. Apparently I was wrong. Just out of curiosity, when did you tamper with my act?"

"Earlier this evening." Lucian had apparently decided that for the moment the only thing to do was to keep talking. "Getting inside the grounds was a snap, Galen. Next time you'll have to introduce better security measures."

Galen nodded almost pleasantly. Ariana swallowed awkwardly, the arm across her throat almost painful. Dear God. What were they going to do to Lucian? All of her fear now was for him. She dug her hands deeper into the pockets of her coat.

"You're quite right," Galen was agreeing easily. "Well, live and learn. The last time I tried this particular operation there weren't any glitches, so I suppose I made the mistake of thinking it was reasonably foolproof."

"There was nothing very brilliant or creative about your apparatus," Lucian growled scornfully. His eyes never left the other magician's face.

"No, but that was part of the beauty of the plan. I believe in the virtues of simplicity, Mr. Hawk." Galen's voice hardened. "I also believe in the virtue of teaching interfering people a lesson that won't soon be forgotten!" He waved the gun in a short arc and instantly the two monks grabbed for Lucian's arms.

He didn't struggle. Lucian stood quietly as they tied his wrists behind his back, his whole attention on Ariana as she watched in horror.

Fury was whipping through Ariana now, and she managed to speak for the first time since Galen's arm had gone around her throat. "What are you going to do?" Her voice was a raw whisper.

"I'm going to see to it that Mr. Hawk thinks twice before he goes around ruining other people's acts!" Galen declared grimly. "This way," he added as his men finished binding Lucian. "I think we want a little more privacy for this, just in case some busybody is still hanging around the parking lot."

Ariana's groping fingers clung to the small gold lipstick case that Drake had given her that morning. She held it tightly within the pocket of the suede jacket as she and Lucian were marched through the hedge to a clearing that was illuminated by a light on top of the fence which encircled the compound.

"Now!"

Without any warning Galen shouted the command. Lucian was hurled back against the wire fence, and Ariana realized what was about to happen. The two men in robes were going to beat him.

"Stop it!" she grated. "Stop it, Galen. You're free to go, for God's sake. What more do you want?"

"Don't panic, my dear. I really don't intend to have him killed. Just made to reconsider the wisdom of his actions!"

The first of the men drew back his fist and launched a solid body blow at Lucian's midsection. Ariana screamed and pulled the gold lipstick case from her pocket. It was now or never. If she waited much longer, Lucian would be bleeding and unconscious. If only Galen didn't have a gun! Grabbing the gun would be the hardest part.

Her scream was ignored by the men as the first blow sent Lucian sagging into the fence. The men who did this kind of work for a living probably expected women to do a lot of screaming. Even Galen didn't seem overly concerned, although he idly shifted his arm to cover her mouth.

But Ariana had the lipstick out of her pocket and was aiming it over her shoulder at her captor's face. Galen was so intent on punishing his other victim that he didn't even see the small object in her hand until it was far too late.

The blinding stream of acid spray flashed into his face.

Instinctively Fletcher Galen yelled and dropped the gun, clawing for his blinded eyes. Ariana had tensed, knowing that she would only have one chance at the weapon before the two toughs at the fence realized what was happening. She dived for it even as Galen stumbled backward, screaming in rage.

She caught the gun just as it struck the ground. Without hesitation she brought it up, leaping away from Galen but focusing the weapon on the two men in robes, who had turned to stare at her.

"Move and I'll shoot!" she said as she edged away from Galen, who had gone to his knees, his hands covering his streaming eyes.

But the two men seemed to know exactly what they were doing. They kept themselves in line with Lucian as they moved forward. "Shoot at us and you'll probably hit your lover," one sneered.

Terrified at that possibility, Ariana tried to edge further to one side. She needed a clear shot and they weren't going to allow her one.

Then the problem was taken out of her hands.

On silent feet Lucian came away from the fence in a menacing rush. Ariana had only time to realize that his hands were free and then he was on the other two men. His fists came down simultaneously at the base of their necks, sending them sprawling forward into the dirt.

"Ariana! The gun!"

She stepped toward him and he swept the wicked instrument out of her hand, turning in one fluid motion to cover the three on the ground. "Honey, why don't you get my glasses for me," he went on softly. "I'd hate to miss and hit someone's chest when I really meant to aim for his shoulder!"

The chilling possibility held the three men on the ground in near stillness, except for Galen who was whimpering softly. Ariana circled the trio warily and scooped up the glasses, which had come off during the rough treatment Lucian had received. She hurried back to him.

"Ah, thank you. That's much better," he drawled, sliding them into place. "Are you okay?"

"Yes! Yes, I'm fine," she managed tightly. "What about you? They hit you so hard, Lucian."

"I'm all right," he assured her, his eyes never wavering from his captives. "Just feeling a bit stupid for not having planned for this contingency."

"How did you get your hands free?" she remembered to ask in amazement.

He grinned. "Magic."

"Lucian! I'm in no mood for jokes!" she stormed furiously, reaction setting in as she realized what a close call they had both had.

"Okay, okay. I'm sorry. It's just that I've learned a lot about rope ties in the course of being a magician. All I needed was to allow a little leeway in the ropes when they tied me, and I accomplished that by tightening the muscles in my hands and wrists while they were busy practicing their Boy Scout techniques. Satisfied?"

"Yes," she groaned.

"So tell me how you managed to incapacitate Galen the way you did," he ordered with grave interest.

Ariana couldn't quite stifle the nervous little smile that sprang to her lips. "Magic."

"Uh huh," he chuckled in mocking admiration. "Some of your brother's magic, perhaps?"

"I'm afraid so. I visited him this morning to see if he could give me some form of protection. He invented that little lipstick for single women alone in the city," she explained.

"Come on, let's get these back to the main building and call the authorities. Your aunt will begin to wonder what's happened to us."

Ariana sighed at the thought of what almost had happened to them as she followed Lucian and his captives back to the now-deserted main building of what had been Fletcher Galen's retreat.

"My eyes," Galen wailed accusingly. "What about my eyes? I need medical help!"

"You'll get it. I'm sure the local police will be glad to take you to a doctor," Lucian shot back uncaringly.

"His eyes will be all right," Ariana whispered. "The effects are only temporary."

It was some time before Ariana and Lucian were free to return to the eagerly awaiting Philomena. The questioning of the local authorities was extensive, and there were papers to be signed. Galen and his men were taken away to the local jail, and Ariana could hear the defeated magician insisting on being allowed to contact his lawyer as the police car drove off.

"The sad part is, he'll probably be back actively pursuing his career within a year," Lucian noted wryly as he at last parked the Jaguar in the small parking lot of the inn.

"Well, at least it won't be at Philomena's expense," Ariana declared in relief. "Thank you, Lucian. I'm sorry my plan got you into danger, though. I've never been so terrified in my life as I was when Galen had his men start beating you!" She shivered at the memory.

Lucian smiled as he took her arm and walked her toward the lobby. "You were brilliant, sweetheart. Remind me to congratulate your brother on that lipstick invention of his! If you hadn't used it when you did, I don't know when I would have gotten the opportunity I needed to deal with those two creeps!"

"Ariana! Lucian!" Philomena was waiting at the lobby entrance, a crowd of former Keepers of the Energy standing curiously behind her. "Thank heavens you're here! We were all so worried when you didn't show up back here, and then when the police called and explained what had happened, we were absolutely shocked! Who would have thought that nice man capable of such things?" She stepped aside and motioned them through the door. "Come inside, come inside. I've already phoned Drake and told him the news. He's on his way up here."

"Tonight?" Ariana asked, startled.

"Well, of course, dear. He wants to know exactly how the lipstick worked in action!"

Lucian was grinning as he followed Philomena into the lobby and threw himself down onto a sofa, pulling Ariana along with him. Galen's former audience gathered close, questions and demands for explanations filling the air.

Patiently Lucian explained everything. A bellhop was dispatched upstairs to bring down the briefcase he'd brought along. When it arrived he opened it up and dug out copies of the documentary evidence the private investigator had had time to find.

"I'm sure there's a lot more than this to be found, but I'm going to call the investigator off the case," Lucian concluded as the newspaper clippings and reports were passed around. "It's the job of the police now. Ariana and I have had enough of the business of exposing fraudulent magicians, haven't we, honey?"

"Definitely!" There was a great deal of feeling in the single word of agreement.

"You two must be exhausted," Philomena finally declared. "Don't feel obliged to stay up while the rest of us rehash our interesting little experience."

"Now that you mention it," Lucian began, getting to his feet, "you have a point, Phil. If you'll excuse us, Ariana and I are going to take your advice."

"What about Drake?" Ariana thought to ask as she was led out of the room.

"You can see him in the morning," Lucian told her bluntly.

Ariana yawned as they started up the staircase. "You know, Lucian, you have a strong, dictatorial tendency. I hope you're not going to try and make a habit out of telling me what to do."

"Oh, I'll probably *try*," he chuckled as he opened the door to their room. "But I doubt whether I'll always succeed. You have your own brand of magic, sweetheart, and it's pretty potent."

"My lipstick?" She smiled sleepily as he took her lightly into his arms.

"No, your magic is real, not mechanical," he murmured urgently. He shook his head, as if slightly dazed. "God, Ariana, when that man held a gun on you and put his arm across your throat..."

She felt his tension and lifted her fingers to stroke the sides of his face. "It's over, Lucian. Believe me, I felt just as sick when I realized what those two men were going to do to you!"

He hugged her close and for a long moment they

simply stood together in the middle of the room, comforting themselves in each other's embrace. And then Lucian gently put her aside and turned to pull back the covers of the bed.

"Never again, honey," he promised fervently as they slowly undressed and made ready for bed. "I'll never let you get that close to danger again. I was so furious with myself for not having realized how dangerous Galen could be! I thought he was just another average con man and most of the professionals steer clear of violence. They make their living by their wits, not with guns."

Ariana looked up at him dreamily, vaguely realizing how exhausted she really was. He bent down and kissed her forehead as he tugged off his shirt. "No fair tempting me with that inviting look of female compliance!"

"Tempting you?" she repeated, yawning again. Her lids were beginning to feel irresistibly heavy, and it was a pleasure to lean against him while he finished the task of undressing her.

"Ummm. What you need tonight after your little adventure is sleep. I'll save my husbandly demands for some other evening."

"Not *husbandly* demands," Ariana remembered to correct sleepily as the last of her clothing fell to the floor and her nightgown was slipped over her head. "We're not married, Lucian."

"Not yet," he agreed, but there was a touch of grim determination in his voice as he lifted her and carried her over to the bed. "We'll discuss that issue in the morning."

"There's nothing to discuss," she tried to explain, but he was already crawling in beside her, pulling her deeply into the curve of his body and cradling her against his chest.

"Go to sleep, Magic Lady."

She did as she was told, allowing sleep to calm the last of her body's tension. The warmth of Lucian's hard, lean frame was as comforting as a fireplace in winter and as protective as a sorceror's magic. Ariana sighed once and gave herself up to it completely.

The morning light filtered through the swaying pines to awaken Ariana slowly and gently. She stretched luxuriously, her toe automatically extending expectantly to find Lucian's bare leg. When she encountered only an empty bed beside her she sat up in rueful annoyance. He seemed to be making a habit out of leaving her to awaken alone when they stayed at this inn!

Last time, she recalled, she had found him downstairs with her aunt. This morning she would probably find him in the same place perhaps along with Drake.

Ariana smiled as she considered how pleased her brother was going to be when she told him how well his "lipstick" had worked. And Aunt Phil would be eagerly awaiting her so that the events of the previous evening could be rehashed once more. And Lucian should be in a pretty good mood, too, Ariana concluded as she showered and dressed for the day. He had held her so tenderly and protectively during the night. Three cheerful, happy faces waiting for her in the sunny dining room. It was going to be a good day.

On that thought Ariana quickly slipped into a dolman-sleeved, diagonally buttoned tunic done in a soft white silky fabric. She paired it with gray pleated trousers. Hastily double-checking her hair in the mirror, she grabbed her room key and headed downstairs to meet her waiting relatives and the man she loved. Her feet, shod in black cuffed suede boots made fast work of the curving staircase.

Ariana came jauntily off the last step, using one hand on the banister to pirouette in the direction of the dining room. Smiling expectantly she sauntered through the open double doors.

But she was not met by the sight of cheerful relatives and an approving lover.

Ariana faltered in surprise at the expression of grim determination which met her on the face of each of the three people waiting for her at the table across the room. Not one of them looked bright or cheerful, she thought vaguely.

Even as she gathered her composure and started forward, Lucian was getting to his feet to meet her halfway. His face looked the grimmest and most determined of the lot, Ariana decided. What on earth had happened?

"Ariana," he greeted her almost formally, "I have

been talking to your family and they and I are agreed. You're not really cut out for an affair. It's okay for some people, but not for you. We've decided you need marriage.'' He drew in his breath and then proclaimed flatly, ''So, I'm going to marry you.''

Ten

As the impact of Lucian's uncompromising statement hit her, Ariana pulled off a little magic of her own. She hid the tremor that went through her and successfully managed a gracious smile. Then, as if politely declining a small gift she said, "Thank you all for being so concerned about me, but there's really no need. I'm quite happy as things are." She took a seat at the breakfast table, ignored the expressions of the other three and reached for the bread basket. "Are there any scones left? I'm starving. Drake, did Lucian tell you how well the lipstick worked? I think you ought to go ahead and patent the chemical spray and the mechanism. It will sell like hotcakes in every big city in the country. A woman can't be too careful these days, you know."

"Which is exactly why I think you ought to consider Lucian's proposal, Ari," her brother shot back relentlessly. "You need a stable, established relationship. You're definitely the careful type!"

"No, I'm not," she contradicted lightly, holding out her cup as the waitress poured coffee. "Not anymore."

"Ariana," Lucian began urgently, "listen to your brother. You've been very cautious for four years. There's no reason to stop now. It's obviously part of your nature!"

"Ari, dear," Philomena interjected in a patiently reasonable tone, "I know Drake and I accused you of being overly careful…"

"And bigoted and prejudiced and several other things which escape me at the moment," Ariana concluded cheerfully. "But that's all changed now. You see before you a new woman. Could you please pass the cream?"

"Damn it, Ariana," Lucian ground out forcefully, "this is no time to go into your stubborn act."

"He's right, Ari," Drake said. "He wants to marry you and I think you should marry him! You're just being stubborn!"

"Am I?"

"Well, of course, you are. What other reason could you have for not accepting Lucian's proposal, dear?" Philomena demanded.

"How about for the simple reason that I haven't been asked?" Ariana bit hungrily into a scone as the other three at the table were stricken with stunned silence.

Lucian managed to break through the barriers of shock first. "Ariana, what the hell's the matter with you? What do you mean you haven't been asked? What do you think I'm doing this morning?"

"*Telling* me to marry you," she explained gently. Poor Lucian. So used to taking what he wanted in life that he hadn't ever learned how to ask for it politely. As his topaz eyes narrowed furiously she gulped another large swallow of coffee and announced to the table in general. "I'm surprised at the three of you. You're all such modern thinkers, but you don't seem to realize that in this modern age women are not told whom to marry. Some man must take the risk of rejection and *ask* the woman of his choice to marry him. Another scone, Philomena?"

"Ariana, listen to me," Drake began heatedly, only to be interrupted by his aunt.

"Ari, dear, you're being ridiculous. Lucian wants to marry you! Why in the world are you choosing this time and place to engage in a game of semantics?"

"You're being stubborn and outrageous and you know it, Ari," Drake charged hotly, glaring at his sister.

It was Lucian who halted the flow of accusations. His body tense and still, he sat staring at Ariana, who met his eyes over the rim of her coffee cup. "No, she's not being stubborn or outrageous or ridiculous," he said slowly, heavily, as if working it all through in his mind. "She just wants me to learn how to take a chance on something that's crucially important to me.''

There was an unnatural silence around the table as Philomena and Drake turned to look at him in astonishment. Ariana broke it by saying very gently, "Is my answer crucially important to you, Lucian?"

He got slowly to his feet and reached down to take her hand. "So important that I haven't got the nerve to ask the question in front of anyone else. Will you please come out into the garden with me, Ariana, while I beg you to marry me?"

Her eyes glowing, Ariana followed him obediently through the lobby and out into the English-style gardens at the rear of the inn. For a long moment they walked in silence. She could feel the tension radiating from him, and part of her longed to soothe and comfort this man who wasn't used to asking for love. But some things had to be done the hard way.

He drew her to a halt beside the fountain, his hands resting lightly at her waist. Never had his eyes seemed so unreadable. Every line of his hard face was grim.

"Ariana, will you please marry me?"

She swallowed tightly. "Why, Lucian?"

He closed his eyes briefly in silent anxiety and then opened them to tell her in a steady, tightly controlled voice, "Because I am so much in love with you that if you don't marry me and come to live with me, I think I will go out of my mind. I need you, sweetheart, in a way I've never needed any other woman. I want you. I can't face the thought of living without you. I know you haven't had a chance yet to fall in love with me, but I can wait. The seeds of your love are there; you couldn't give yourself to me the way you do if they weren't. You wouldn't have put up with me this long if you didn't feel something for me. For God's sake, honey, put me out of my misery and tell me you'll marry me!''

Ariana lifted her hands to cup his tortured face, her own expression full of the love she had been masking all morning with flippancy. "Of course, I'll marry you, Lucian. I've loved you from that first night here at the inn.''

He blinked, catlike, looking down at her with wonder and surprise. "You love me?'' His fingers probed her waist in a small, urgent movement. *"You love me?''* he repeated, dazed.

She nodded, smiling gently. "Yes.''

Lucian groaned and swept her tightly against him. "Sweetheart!'' he growled hoarsely into her hair. "Sweetheart, you won't ever be sorry, I swear it. I didn't even understand what it meant to be in love, much less how to ask for it in return before I met you. Now I couldn't survive without it and I would be willing to beg for it! My God, Ariana. Oh, my God, how I love you!''

The two figures by the fountain were still entwined in each other's arms when Philomena and Drake eventually risked a peek from the window in the lobby. Drake grinned in satisfaction and his aunt smiled with blissful assurance.

"I can't quite figure out which of them has the

other wrapped around his or her little finger,'' Drake chuckled.

"That's what makes it a perfect relationship,'' Philomena explained in satisfaction. "When things are that perfect, a couple might as well marry.'' She turned away from the window with a distant look in her sparkling eyes. "Now, let's see. They'll be needing a little interior decorating for their new home, don't you think? I wonder how Lucian feels about the color red.''

*   *   *   *   *

#1 New York Times bestselling author

NORA ROBERTS

introduces the loyal and loving, tempestuous and tantalizing Stanislaski family.

Coming in November 2000:

The Stanislaski Brothers
Mikhail and Alex

Their immigrant roots and warm, supportive home had made Mikhail and Alex Stanislaski both strong and passionate. And their charm makes them irresistible....

In February 2001, watch for
THE STANISLASKI SISTERS: Natasha and Rachel

And a brand-new Stanislaski story from Silhouette Special Edition,
CONSIDERING KATE

Available at your favorite retail outlet.

Silhouette®
Where love comes alive™

Coming in November 2000
Based on the bestselling continuity series

An original
Silhouette Christmas Collection

36
HOURS:

THE CHRISTMAS
THAT CHANGED
EVERYTHING

With stories by

MARY LYNN BAXTER
MARILYN PAPPANO
CHRISTINE FLYNN

'TIS THE SEASON...
WHERE TIME IS OF THE ESSENCE
IN THE SEARCH FOR TRUE LOVE!

Available at your favorite retail outlet.

Where love comes alive™

Visit Silhouette at www.eHarlequin.com   PS36

You're not going to believe this offer!

In October and November 2000, buy any two Harlequin or Silhouette books and save $10.00 off future purchases, or buy any three and save $20.00 off future purchases!

Just fill out this form and attach 2 proofs of purchase (cash register receipts) from October and November 2000 books and Harlequin will send you a coupon booklet worth a total savings of $10.00 off future purchases of Harlequin and Silhouette books in 2001. Send us 3 proofs of purchase and we will send you a coupon booklet worth a total savings of $20.00 off future purchases.

Saving money has never been this easy.

I accept your offer! Please send me a coupon booklet:

Name: _____

Address: _____ City: _____

State/Prov.: _____ Zip/Postal Code: _____

Optional Survey!

In a typical month, how many Harlequin or Silhouette books would you buy <u>new</u> at retail stores?

☐ Less than 1   ☐ 1   ☐ 2   ☐ 3 to 4   ☐ 5+

Which of the following statements best describes how you <u>buy</u> Harlequin or Silhouette books? Choose one answer only that <u>best</u> describes you.

☐ I am a regular buyer and reader
☐ I am a regular reader but buy only occasionally
☐ I only buy and read for specific times of the year, e.g. vacations
☐ I subscribe through Reader Service but also buy at retail stores
☐ I mainly borrow and buy only occasionally
☐ I am an occasional buyer and reader

Which of the following statements best describes how you <u>choose</u> the Harlequin and Silhouette series books you buy <u>new</u> at retail stores? By "series," we mean books within a particular line, such as *Harlequin PRESENTS* or *Silhouette SPECIAL EDITION*. Choose one answer only that <u>best</u> describes you.

☐ I only buy books from my favorite series
☐ I generally buy books from my favorite series but also buy books from other series on occasion
☐ I buy some books from my favorite series but also buy from many other series regularly
☐ I buy all types of books depending on my mood and what I find interesting and have no favorite series

Please send this form, along with your cash register receipts as proofs of purchase, to:
In the U.S.: Harlequin Books, P.O. Box 9057, Buffalo, NY 14269
In Canada: Harlequin Books, P.O. Box 622, Fort Erie, Ontario L2A 5X3
(Allow 4-6 weeks for delivery) Offer expires December 31, 2000.

PHQ4002